John J Waller

Prize Essays

Chiefly Shaksperean studies

John J Waller

Prize Essays
Chiefly Shaksperean studies

ISBN/EAN: 9783337424466

Printed in Europe, USA, Canada, Australia, Japan

Cover: Foto ©Andreas Hilbeck / pixelio.de

More available books at **www.hansebooks.com**

PRIZE ESSAYS:

CHIEFLY

SHAKSPEREAN STUDIES.

"In the discovery of truth, in the developement of man's mental powers and privileges, each generation has its assigned part; and it is for us to endeavour to perform our portion of this perpetual task of our species."—WHEWELL.

CHIEFLY

SHAKSPEREAN STUDIES.

BY

JOHN J. WALLER,

Editor of "The University College of Wales Magazine," Sylvester Petyt Scholar of the Skipton Grammar School, Prize-man of the New Shakspere Society, Fellow of the Royal Society of Literature.

———————

ABERYSTWYTH:
J. GIBSON, "CAMBRIAN NEWS" PRINTING WORKS, MILL STREET.

MDCCCLXXXII.

"The honour of great names 'tis just to guard;
They are a trust but lent us, which we take,
And should, in reverence to the donor's fame,
With care transmit them down to other hands."

SHIRLEY.

THESE ESSAYS ARE RESPECTFULLY

Dedicated

To the Right Honourable LORD ABERDARE

(PRESIDENT OF THE COUNCIL),

LEWIS MORRIS, Esq., M.A.

(SECRETARY OF THE COUNCIL),

The Rev. T. C. EDWARDS, M.A.

(PRINCIPAL),

Of the UNIVERSITY COLLEGE OF WALES.

"I look upon every true thought as a valuable acquisition to society, which cannot possibly hurt or obstruct the good effect of any other truth whatsoever for they all partake of one common essence, and necessarily coincide with each other; and, like the drops of rain which fall separately into the river, mix themselves at once with the stream, and strengthen the general current."

DR. MIDDLETON.

INDEX.

—

"Go, little booke ; God send thee good passage,
And specially let this be thy prayere,
Unto them all that thee will read or hear,
Where thou art wrong after their help to call,
Thee to correct in any part, or all."

CHAUCER.

FORESPEECH.

It is very difficult to write an Introduction—such a thing is generally looked upon as a superfluity, stale, flat, and unprofitable. It has been likened to "a pilaster put upon the face of a building for look's sake," and to a "Caryatid holding upon her head a structure which she did not build, and which could stand just as well without her support." But if one will persist in blotting and spoiling good paper, and in sending out to the world some sort of a book, I suppose one must either justify the presumption, or make some apology for it. Perhaps I may do both.

Somebody has said that it is a very laudable ambition, the wish to bring into the world a new book—a thing that can speak as soon as it is born (that is, if the world will only let it!). Unfortunately, a man cannot do that. No doubt it is a praiseworthy desire, but at the same time it is a very serious matter, this bringing forth of intellectual offspring. Witness to the pangs and throes with which it has been produced, the parental partiality with which it has been welcomed when born in secret, and the fond affection which follows it still! Who can understand (save members of the craft) the tremulous anxiety of this young intellectual father?—the hopes and fears, the thoughts and dreams that hover around his child; the yearnings, and the heartfelt wishes that accompany its sending out into the world; the palpitating apprehensions, the strange mixture of fear and impatience with which the decision and sentence of its readers are anticipated—the decree of those who will either return it with scorn and ridicule, or send it on to other friends with the dignity and honour of a reasonable production.* Truly, no fond

---

Compare Binney's lecture (Exeter Hall series) on "Authorship."

mother could be more sensible of such feelings than the young
aspirant to literary fame :

> " None but an author knows an author's cares,
> Or Fancy's fondness for the child she bears."

"Come, come, that's enough : no more of your idle dreamings!"
you say. But, "my gentle reader" (for you must allow me to
address you by this familiar title), as for you, I know you well, and
perhaps can say more about you than you would care to say about
yourself—revealing virtues which your modesty would veil, and
feelings which your reticence would hide. Do I not know of your
kindness in the past to another ward of mine?*—the interest you
had manifested in its infancy—the loyal love that looked so
anxiously for its periodical visits—the pious care that perused its
every word—the devotion that made it your pride and pleasure to
contribute with uncomplaining punctuality whatever was necessary
for its welfare and support? Ah! I see at once the conscious blush
upon your face owns all my praises true. What, then, have I to
fear? Surely you will extend your favours towards this finer and
better nourished specimen of intellectual offspring! I know you are
my friend, faithful and just to me, so I have little need to pray for
your leniency, since you know that I myself am, as yet, but a
beardless boy. Still I am sure there are some amongst you, dear
readers, who like to find fault, or to criticize, as you prefer to call
it. Let me warn you before you say a word, not to intermeddle
with affairs or works which in no way concern you, for unless you
produce the written authority by which you are constituted judges,
I shall most assuredly decline to plead to your jurisdiction. But I
think I hear you reply that an author ought to try to please
everybody –like the honest man who keeps the public "ordinary,"
at which all persons are welcome, provided they pay their money,
and if everything is not agreeable to their taste, however nice and
whimsical that may be, will challenge the right to censure—and
abuse if they like. Yes, I hear what you say, but I would rather
have you consider me as the modest, good natured individual who

provides a private or eleemosynary treat for his more intelligent
friends, with a fare depreciated by the mob, and not intended for
them. How can you, then, find fault? Why, your good-breeding
forbids it, and despite yourself, you are forced to approve, and even
commend whatever is set before you, whether you like it or not.*

It is generally understood that if a reader is to have a thorough
appreciation of a writer's thoughts, he cannot do better than put
himself somewhat into the position of the writer when such thoughts
were transmitted to paper. I have little apprehension that anything
in these essays will not be thoroughly understood; nor have I any
extraordinary statement to make in connection with the writing of
them—as, for instance, Swift, who, to assist the reader in so delicate
an affair as the proper appreciation of all that is sublime and witty
in him, thinks it his duty to say that the shrewdest pieces of his
treatise were conceived in bed in a garret; at other times he had
thought fit to sharpen his intention with hunger, and in general the
whole work was begun, continued, and ended under a long course of
physic, and *a great want of money*—though I can heartily apply this
last remark; yet, I think it necessary to explain the circumstances
under which these Essays were written, together with some justification for publishing them. Some of them have appeared elsewhere,
and I reprint them here with little or no alteration, though not
without some reluctance; but to re-construct them entirely would
entail too much labour. The short Essays on "Style and Thought"
and "The Decline of the Drama" must necessarily be looked upon as
meagre and unfinished. being first efforts in collegiate competition,
but since they were awarded first place in the class lists, I am led to
include them. In the first mentioned the remarks will no doubt
appear dogmatic and paradoxical, but it must be borne in mind that
this is simply an attempt to prove that there is truth in Buffon's
famous aphorism, "The style is the man." A rejoinder and some
remarks thereon have now been added.

The bulk of this book, however, consists of Shaksperean studies
upon subjects given out for competition amongst the students of the
University College of Wales, by the New Shakspere Society. I can

Compare Henry Fielding's Introduction to "Tom Jones."

only look with pleasure upon the labour spent in the making of these Essays, and from the way in which they had been received by the examiner, the press, and others, together with the fact that the subjects are entirely new,—this being the first attempt at any collected account of "Shakspere's Hypocrites" or "Shakspere's Clowns"* yet published—I am emboldened to print them and send them forth to friends. And I shall be well repaid for all the trouble taken if those who peruse them find as much pleasure in reading as I have had in investigating; or even if they are the means of sending a single enquirer to the pages of the poet to study for himself. For what depths and heights have we in Shakspere to explore! — no man ever fathomed deeper; no man ever soared higher; no human being using the best weapons of intellectual accomplishment ever accomplished so much,—he stands on the very pinnacle of fame in intellectual attainment. Listen to his companion dramatist :—

> "Triumph, my Britain! thou hast one to show,
> To whom all scenes of Europe homage owe.
> *He was not for an age, but for all time!*
> And all the muses still were in their prime,
> When, like Apollo, he came forth to warm
> Our ears, or like a Mercury to charm!
> Nature herself was proud of his designs,
> And joyed to wear the dressing of his lines!
> Yet, must I not give Nature all; thy art,
> My gentle Shakspere must enjoy a part,
> For, though the poet's matter nature be,
> His art doth give the fashion . . . . .
> . . . . . Look, how the father's face
> Lives in his issue, even so the race
> Of Shakspere's mind and manners brightly shines
> In his well torned and true filed lines.
> Sweet Swan of Avon! what a sight it were
> To see thee in our waters yet appear,
> And make those flights upon the banks of Thames,
> That so did take Eliza and our James!
> But stay! I see thee in the hemisphere
> Advanc'd, and made a constellation there!

This is not quite correct, for I find that an essay on *The Clowns and Fools of Shakspere* has been written by Douce, though I have not been able to see it, and it is now out of print.

Shine forth thou *Star of Poets*, and with rage,
Or influence, chide or cheer the drooping stage,
Which, since thy flight from hence, hath mourned like night,
And despairs day, but for thy volumes light."

In conclusion, I beg to acknowledge with gratitude the able and judicious criticism of Prof. MacCallum, M.A., when these Essays were first submitted to him ; the kindness of Prof. Angus, M.A., for several happy hints ; and to thank most sincerely those whose names appear in the list of subscribers at the end of the book, for their help in defraying the cost of printing and publishing.

University College of Wales,
June, 1882.

From Ben Jonson's poem in the folio of 1623—"To the memory of my beloved, the AUTHOR WILLIAM SHAKESPEARE : and what he hath left us."—Ben Jonson's works, page 693.

SHAKSPERE'S HYPOCRITES.

THE NEW SHAKSPERE SOCIETY offer annually a valuable prize of books, for open competition, at the University College of Wales, for the best essay upon a Shaksperean subject. The following essay was awarded the prize in 1881.

THE HYPOCRITES OF SHAKSPERE.

"A Hypocrite is good for nothing but sight."—PERICLES

"Thy very looks are lies;
Eternal falsehood smiles in thy lips, and flashes in thine eyes."
SMITH.

"A man who stole the livery of the Court of Heaven to serve the devil in."—POLLOCK.

E might wish for a more genial subject than the detested quality of hypocrisy in the works of our greatest dramatist, but we could not wish for a better, since its consideration will involve the study of some of our favourite author's most forcible creations. Moreover, these rogues, these villains of Shakspere are amongst the characters he liked most to portray; he takes delight in uniting great intellectual vigour, great mental power, with physical deformity or moral depravity, and in giving them success over the forces of the world and the powers of men brought in contact with them. But Shakspere has been blamed for his villains; it is said that he displays in them pictures too disgusting, pictures which harrow up the mind unmercifully, and torture the senses beyond the limit. It is true that our poet paints for us some hideous portraits, but after all they are human, they are natural. He never "varnishes over wild and blood-thirsty passions with a pleasant exterior, never clothes crime, and want of principle with a false show of greatness of soul," and surely he is not to be blamed for this—he is rather to be praised. If the pictures are revolting and distasteful, we shall hate them the more as we meet them in real life, but if sin be varnished over we are all the more likely to fall victims to its beguiling snares.

The universality of Shakspere's work is everywhere manifest. He does not content himself with a picture of one side of life; he gives us every phase of it, every diversity of rank, sex, and age—from the dawnings of infancy to feeblest old age ; the king and the beggar, the hero and the pickpocket, the savage and the idiot, the warrior and the coward. And he not only paints men and women, he shades out also the world of spirits, summons before us the midnight ghost; he peoples the air with winged sylphs, the beauteous groves with sportive fairies, the black and blasted heath with weird and sexless witches ; and all this is described with such wonderful power and truth, that we believe, if such beings existed, they would act and speak just as the poet has made them. This great truth of conception distinguishes our poet from the rest of the dramatists of his own age, or indeed from those of any age.

So too may be noticed his gradual development of character in its sphere of action. His men and women are not like those of Marlowe, or of Ben Johnson, with one fixed characteristic, one great ruling passion, begun and carried out all through the play. Shakspere's characters grow in goodness or in crime as the action proceeds. We can form some estimate of them, we can often say a great deal about them, but when we have said all, we feel that something remains which we cannot fully understand, some hidden mystery underlying which we cannot explain—in short we feel that they are like ourselves, that they are natural, and being natural we know we can never get at their full meaning.

This quality of hypocrisy, although it may not be so unattractive, allows the poet full scope for his power, as the analysis of the different types of hypocrisy in his characters is a very difficult thing. He has not merely to analyse a real, natural man, he has to analyse a mask which a man puts on ; and as a mask can be assumed in so many different ways, so Shakspere gives us a great many different varieties of hypocrites. For instance, we shall have to speak of Richard III., and his hypocrisy used to satisfy a boundless ambition for the crown ; of Iago, with his ensnaring trap to accomplish his revenge, and to satisfy his love for dangerous action ; of Edmund, with the characteristics of both—he is a villain and a traitor combined. Then, there is Buckingham—a faint shadow of his master Richard III. and his ambition; and King John, the hard-hearted tyrant, without any of the refined feelings of human nature. There is Falstaff, too, whose hypocrisy is of quite a different kind—devoid of serious crime, malice, or envy ; and Parolles, of the same type, but without any of Falstaff's sparkling wit, frankness, and good fellowship. He is simply a selfish, deceitful, inventive scoundrel. Angelo is of another type— hypocrisy used in the service of self-love by one who has an exaggerated idea of his own goodness ; a man aspiring to honour, dignity, and political power, and to be a saint in moral life; but in the hour of temptation, he is found to be as false and tyrannical in the one, as he is hypocritical and base in the other. And lastly, we shall notice the female hypocrites—Goneril and Regan, prompted by their selfish desire, their covetousness for their father's land and power.

In the consideration of our subject we shall take the characters in the chronological order of the plays—following the "Leopold Shakspere," the text from which all quotations are given.

RICHARD III.

ALLUSION IN CHRISTOPHER BROOKE (1614).*

I.

My tongue in firie dragon's spleene I steepe,
That acts, with accents, cruelty may found;

Part 1. Stanza viii.

II.

To him that impt my fame with Clio's quill,
Whose magick rais'd me from oblivion's den;
That writ my story on the Muses hill,
And with my actions dignifi'd his pen:
He that from Helicon sends many a rill,
Whose nectared veines are drunke by thirstie men;
  Crown'd be his stile with fame, his head with bayes;
  And none detract, but gratulate his praise.

Yet, if his scenes have not engrost all grace,
The much-fam'd action could extend on stage.

Part 2. Stanzas i. ii.

III.

My working head (my counsell's consistory)
Debates how I might raigne, the princes living:

Ibid. Stanza xxvi.

The devlish fury in my brest entends
In spite of danger and all opposite barrs;
  To cut this knot the mistick fates conteyne,
  And set my life and kingdom on this mayne.

Part 3. Stanza xxxviii.

---

* From the Poems of Christopher Brooke. The Ghost of Richard III. expressing himself in three parts— (1) His character, (2) his legend, (3) his tragedie. Reprinted from *Shakspere's Centurie of Prayse,* New Shakspere Society's papers, 1879, pp. 109.

RICHARD III.

Tetchy and wayward was thy infancy,
Thy school-days frightful, desperate, wild, and furious,
Thy prime of manhood daring, bold, and venturous,
Thy age confirmed, proud, subtle, sly, and bloody :
More mild and yet more harmful, kind in hatred.
Act. IV. iv. 169—173.

Richard III. is the first great drama in which Shakspere
proves himself to be the first great genius of his time.
Although it is written upon the plan of Marlowe, whose
great characteristic was to portray the workings of a single
passion in a character—as, for instance, in Dr. Faustus, the
lust of dominion—yet, the Richard III. of Shakspere is far
more complex, he is described with far more precision and
power than the characters of the earlier dramatist. The
great idea of the play is to set forth the dangers of a supreme
personal genius which enacts the laws of society and the
world, and the weakness of a mediocre talent which respects
those laws. The nation has just survived a period of great
disorder, suffering, and loss—disasters so often resulting
from dependence upon the passion and power of despotic
kings. The Civil War has at last been closed by the
victory of the House of York, but there is still universal
unquiet and dissatisfaction. The position of things was such,
says the Chronicler, and the temper of men such that no
one can say whom he ought to trust, and whom he ought to

fear; there was a universal birth of hostility, hypocrisy, and dissimulation ; there was a ripe field for intrigues and sneaking wickedness which had grown up luxuriantly in a sudden change to peace and Circean luxury at court. "The natural and usual close of such a period of fierce and demoralizing contention is the absolute decline of all to the ambition that unites activity, boldness, and sagacity, with hypocrisy, unscrupulousness, and selfishness in extremest developement."

At this period Richard of Glo'ster comes forward with all his self-confidence and superior endowments of mind, and with his great insight into the weakness and inability of the "simpletons" around him. The historian, Sir Thos. More— the source, through *Holinshed's Chronicle* of Shakspere's *Richard III.*—says that Richard was the third son, and in wit and courage was equal with either of his brothers (Edward and Clarence), in body and prowess far under them both. He was born with teeth in his mouth ; he was little of stature, ill-featured of limbs, crookbacked, his left shoulder much higher than his right, and hard featured of visage. He was malicious, envious, wrathful, and ever froward. He was close and secret, a great dissimuler, lowly of countenance, arrogant of heart, outwardly compinable where he inwardly hated, not letting to kiss where he thought to kill, dispiteous and cruel, not for evil will always, but often for ambition, and ever for the surety and increase of his estate. Friend or foe was indifferent, where his advantage grew he spared no man's death whose life withstood his purpose. The Richard of Shakspere is said to be a modification of this picture, but he could scarcely be blacker, more fierce and terrible, than our poet has depicted him.

Richard is incarnate ambition itself, and he devotes it all to one great end—the seizure of the English Crown—

"I'll make my heaven to dream upon the Crown."

Ambition is the main spring of his actions; to obtain greatness and power is his object, and hypocrisy is the great instrument in his hand for its attainment. He is quite as ambitious as Macbeth, but his ambition is of a different quality. Macbeth was fascinated with the gaudy glitter and pomp of royalty ; Richard's desire was for power, not pomp—"to command, check, o'erbear all that are of better person than myself." He desires not only to be great, but to be greater than anybody else : and to gain his end he commits the most horrible crimes, he has no scruples, and he is always successful so long as there is a goal to aim at,— it is when he has murdered all his friends and overcome all the forces that are against him that he fails.

Like Edmund *(King Lear)* feels the brand of "base" and "bastard," so Richard feels keenly his distorted and misshapen form. It wounds his pride, it irritates his spite, and he makes this deformity the plea for cherishing a deep-rooted hatred against all who are more comely than himself—

I that am curtailed of this fair proportion,
Cheated of feature by dissembling nature,
Deformed, unfinished, sent before my time
Into this breathing world, scarce half made up,
And that so lamely and unfashionable,
That dogs bark at me as I halt by them—

I am determined to prove a villain.
Act I. i. 18—30.

And his outward misshapen body reflects his inward villainous nature. He has no pity in his heart, he has no love, nor has he any fear; to him conscience is a word for cowards, and by the strength of his will putting it aside he ruthlessly sheds the blood of those who should have been his nearest and dearest friends.   Deeds of blood are to him songs of sweet music, and a dozen lives weight but lightly on his depraved and villainous soul.   He does not hesitate a moment, nor think long upon the means he will employ to effect his purpose.   He determines to "hew his way out with a bloody axe" to the Crown, and we must confess that he carries out his resolve right faithfully.

But despite his outward deformity, Richard is conscious of his great intellectual superiority and high birth—

> I was born so high,
> Our aëry buildeth on the Cedar's top,
> And dallies with the wind, and scorns the sun.

He treats the rest of mankind with contempt; he regards them all as good-natured inoffensive simpletons; the subtlest statesmen are to him mere bunglers—mere tools for his special use.   Richard is a warrior, too, of unequivocal valour; his bravery is unquestioned, and he has that in his character which is most at variance with hypocrisy.   His delight is in the battle field, but now he says—

> Grim-visag'd war has smoothed his wrinkled front,
> And now instead of mounting barbed steeds,
> To fright the soul of fearful adversaries,
> He capers nimbly in the ladies chamber
> To the lascivious pleasing of a lute.
>
> *Act I. i. 9—13.*

He hates the idle pleasures of these days, he feels his occupation gone, and how uninformed he is in deeds of love. so he is determined to prove himself a villain.

It is in hypocrisy, however, that Richard is most accomplished ; as a dissembler he is most profound :

> Why I can smile, and murther whiles I smile,
> And cry content to that which grieves my heart,
> And wet my face with artificial tears,
> And frame my face to all occasions.

He is very fond of using religious expressions, as if determined to prostitute to the service of hell a religion which he inwardly abjured : while he is in " body and soul a devil, he can appear like an angel of light." We see him at one time in affecting humility, at another in decoying amiability ; to-day a foul murderer, to-morrow a pious and saintly penitent ; he has the double guise of a passionate and raging tyrant, and of a sweet and honied lover ; he makes men believe he is persecuted and maltreated, while at the same time he is undermining and plotting the death of everybody around him. As Furnival has pointed out, Richard's hypocrisies, his exultations in them, his despising and insulting of his victims, his grim humour, and delight in gulling fools, and in his own villany—all this is very forcibly brought out no less than thirteen times in the play.

His first victim is Clarence, whom he has determined to set in dead hatred against the king. Richard has been instrumental in having Clarence put in prison, and then he promises very feelingly to do all he can to get the victim released. But he never intends to do anything of the kind—

> Simple plain Clarence, I do love thee so
> That I will shortly send thy soul to Heaven.
> *Act I. Sc. i. 118—120.*

He destroys his brother, and glories in his treachery ; beweeps the cause to his friends—"simple gulls," as he calls

them—quotes scripture, and then goes to plan another
wicked scheme.   His next dupe is Hastings.   He makes
his friend believe how grievously he feels the King's illness,
but his selfish wish when alone is something different—

> God take king Edward to his mercy,
> And leave the world for me to bustle in.
>> *Act I. Sc. ii. 150—151.*

But Richard is most proud of his power to deceive and
fascinate women by his hypocrisy and honied tongue, and
judging from his astonishing success in this direction, he
places a just estimate upon his ability.   The courtship
scene with Lady Anne is one of the most striking examples
of the extent of his wily power.   Here he brings the whole
of his resources into play; personal attractiveness he has
none—but action, voice, and eye, these he uses with the cleverness of an accomplished actor.   He approaches the young and
beautiful widow at first boldly, quite confident of success,
but finding her not so easily overcome, he turns penitent,
and tells her that her beauty was the sole cause of the
murder of her father, Henry VI.   He had never shed a
tear for anything but her beauty.   At first the Lady Anne
scorns his flattery, but his wily arts prevail, and his
hypocrisy reaches its climax when he bares his breast, gives
her his sword, and bids her

> Let forth the soul that adoreth thee,
> I lay it naked to the deadly stroke,
> And humbly beg the death on bended knee.
>> *Act I. Sc. ii. 176—178.*

She yields to his desires, and with this triumph Richard
gets more contempt for man than ever.   He laughs in his

sleeve, and is himself astonished that a lady could be wooed and won in such a humour. But he will not keep her long—he who has killed her husband, and her father cannot rest satisfied with even this victory. She, too, must make room for another to suit his wicked purpose.

His next piece of hyprocrisy is before Queen Elizabeth, Hastings, and Dorset. He complains that they do him wrong to say that he does not love the King and Queen. Because he cannot flatter and speak fair, smile in men's faces and deceive them, he must be held a rancorous enemy. He pretends to be ignorant of his brother's imprisonment, believes himself disgraced, and all the nobility held in contempt. How truly he reveals his own character in professing to be what he is not !

> I would to God my heart were flint like Edward's,
> Or Edward's soft and pitiful like mine,
> I am too childish-foolish for this world.
> *Act I. Sc. iii. 139—142.*

His friends advise him to be revenged of Rivers, Vaughan, and Grey, he quotes Scriptures in reply, and tells them that " God bids us do good for evil." He continues his art with King Edward on his death-bed. He pleads forgiveness for anything done unwittingly, or in rage. He wants to be friendly with everybody, for it is as death to him to be at enmity : he hates it, and desires all good men's love. In fact he does not know that there is an Englishman alive with whom his soul is any jot at odds ; and to crown it all he thanks God for his humility. Then he announces the death of Clarence—Clarence, his brother, so cruelly murdered—in the coolest manner possible ; and with what heartlessness does he try to shift the blame from himself to the Queen? To the children of Clarence the hypocrite goes and weeps, as the lad afterwards tells us,

> And when my uncle told me so he wept,
> And pitied me, and kiss'd my cheek,
> Bade me rely on him as on my father,
> And he would love me truly as his child.
>
> *Act II. Sc. iii. 18—20.*

He craves a blessing from his mother on his knees, and when it is given him he says " Amen ! and make me die a good old man." The young prince, Edward V., goes to Richard in his sorrow for loss of friends, little knowing that he is standing before their very murderer. The villain comforts him, and warns him against his uncles in language which could be most fittingly applied to himself :—

> The uncles which you want were dangerous ;
> Your grace attended to their sugar'd words ;
> But look not on the poison of their hearts ;
> God keep you from them ; and from such false friends.
>
> *Act III. i. 12—15.*

One of Richard's finest strokes is the scene in which he leads Hastings into the trap for his own destruction. And he does this at a time when Hastings thinks himself most secure, and in a manner which would lead him to think he was Richard's most trusted friend. But he has to die for his faithfulness, and when his head is produced, Richard declares—

> So dear I loved him that I must weep,
> I took him for the plainest, harmless creature
> That breathed upon the earth a Christian.
>
> *Act III. Sc. v. 23—25.*

He deceives the Mayor too in the same way ; and sends Buckingham to make that most brutal and base insinuation of his mother's adultery. Then he resolves himself upon the murder of the two princes—"now will I go and draw the brats of Clarence out of sight." He has now reached the goal of his ambition, the Crown, and Buckingham goes to address the courtiers and citizens on his behalf—to tell the people what a good old man Richard is, that he is not "lolling on his lude day-bed," but meditating with two deep divines. The pretended saint then appears to the crowd from the balcony above, between two bishops—"two props of virtue for a Christian prince"—with a book of prayer in his hand. They press him to take the crown, but with well feigned reluctance, he pretends how unwilling he is to accept such a heavy responsibility. He cannot tell why so many good citizens should have disturbed him from his earnest in the service of his God. He pleads his unfitness for royalty; he cannot, and will not yield to them in accepting the crown. But after more sham persuasion on the part of his dupe, Buckingham, the hypocrite tells them that his heart is not made of stone; he will yield to their entreaties, though against his conscience and his soul, and he prays for patience to endure the load.

The scene in which Richard broaches to Buckingham his desire for the death of the princes is one of those which our poet could so forcibly picture. We shall have to notice similar and more powerful scenes in *King John* and *Othello*, where the villains, by mere suggestion, make known their purpose, and excite their dupes to immediate action. But Buckingham is staggered at Richard's hint of "Death!"— he must have breathing time before he can commit such an arch deed of piteous massacre. Richard, however, is not a man to shrink from anything, be it the bloodiest deed possible, and he is sharp in his resolve that "the deep-revolving, witty Buckingham, no more shall be the

B

neighbour of my counsels." We marvel how he can go on from one black deed to another so rapidly, for no sooner he has despatched his two nephews, and banished Buckingham, than he resolves that his wife must die. He orders Catesby to give it out abroad that she is sick, for he must speedily be married to his brother's daughter that his ill-gotten kingdom may be more secure.

Away he goes on his mission, and thinks himself a "jolly thriving wooer." He is intercepted in his mission by his mother and Queen Elizabeth, mother to the beautiful maiden he now resolves to wed. The Queen demands from him her children, whom he has so ruthlessly slain, and Richard sets himself to work at the difficult task of gaining her to compliance with his vile wishes. He renews with her the honied words which were so successful with Anne. This villain who has murdered her children, and almost all her relations, has the deep-rooted hypocrisy to plead that he did it all for the love of her daughter. It is as if he profaned and insulted this his last sanctuary of refuge; we feel that he must have run the length of his wickedness, and that this, his crowning piece of villainy, must bring down his blood upon his head. His well-affected kiss to the Queen is followed by the expression of his real self—

> Relenting fool, and shallow, changing woman,
> *Act IV. iv. 432.*

showing how contemptuously he regarded mankind when he had made it serve his purpose.

But his end comes at last. Such wickedness, treachery, and hypocrisy will bring their reward in one way or another. Richard is upset by the landing of Richmond, the great avenger, yet he is confident in himself and his own strong will; but his conscience—and we have often wondered where it was—now demands to be heard. This involuntary force, this voice of God, which he has all through his life time bound down within him, now rises up against him. As the spirits of those so pitilessly murdered appear before him in his dream, the thousand tongues of conscience remind him of their many warnings throughout his career. He who has denied the existence of any higher power than himself; he who has stamped out every feeling of pity, every spring of love and tenderness from his heart; who, by his hypocrisy, has deceived Heaven itself, at last gives way before this supernatural power—-

> Guilty, guilty!
> I shall despair—there is no creature loves me,
> And if I die, no soul shall pity me:—
> Nay, wherefore, should they since that I myself
> Find in myself no pity to myself.
> *Act V. iii. 201—205.*

But the day of the battle comes, and Richard regains his self-reliance : it was only when half awake that he felt intimidated, and in addressing his forces he calls conscience a word for cowards only; again he puts his confidence in his strong arm, and bids them—

> March on again bravely, let us to 't pell-mell,
> If not to Heaven, then hand in hand to hell.
> *Act V. iii. 314—315.*

He calls Richmond a "milksop," a man who has never felt as much cold "as over shoes in snow;" and it is Richard's humiliation to Richmond which is the great secret of his fall. The fact that he, the Richard who has overcome everything, conquered the very forces of the world; he, who has been too much for everybody, made them all instruments to his hand, and never failed, should be overcome by a

"mere milksop," is more than he can bear. He feels how
lonely he is, he has murdered all his friends, he has attained
his unworthy end; but now his mighty intellect becomes
over-clouded, his warlike dexterity, as if conscious that it
was misplaced in so great a hypocrite, deserts him—he
descends from the valiant soldier to the doomed desperado,
and he falls a victim to his long practised treachery.

BUCKINGHAM.

The Duke of Buckingham is a faint reflection of Richard's
ambition, and of his hypocrisy. He tells us that he too

> Can counterfeit the deep tragedian,
> Speak and look back, and pry on every side,—
> Tremble and start at the wagging of a straw,
> Intending deep suspicion; ghastly looks
> Are at my service, like enforced smiles;
> And both are ready in their offices
> At any time to grace my stratagems.
> *Act III. v. 5—11.*

He promises to use, and does use all these powers to help
Richard to the throne; and in return he is to receive the
Earldom of Hereford. Of course Richard dupes him, and
Buckingham, who has been one of his best friends, looses
his head for his faithfulness. Like Richard, Buckingham
feels remorse of conscience; the "high all-seer," whom he
has so shamefully wronged, visits him also, and turns his
hypocrisy to his own destruction.

KING JOHN.

"O! when the last account 'twixt Heaven and earth
Is to be made, then shall this hand and seal
Witness against us to damnation.
How oft the sight of means to do ill deeds
Makes ill deeds done!"

Act IV. ii. 216—220.

KING JOHN.

In "King John," Shakspere strikes out in a new direction,
he does not here devote the whole play to one prominent
character with one great ruling passion: we have a group of
fine characters moving round a subtle tyrant. Constance is
a new figure with our poet,—a passionate, sorrowing mother,
the very essence of maternal tenderness and love. Then
there is Arthur, who moves about with a pathetic beauty,
gentleness, and innocence—like a lamb amongst ravening
wolves. The most serious and poignant phases of the play
are relieved by the accompaniment of the comic character
in Falconbridge, who begins in Shakspere a kind of humour
which the poet knows so well how to blend with his more
terrible characters. Falconbridge is a typical Englishman
with his courage, frankness, and national pride. The
Bastard, too, with his bluff, out-spoken manner, contributes
much to the relief of the play.

The poet here unites all the evils of a disputed succession ;
society is only in a semi-barbarous state, a time when the
King is vested with more power than he can safely wield

without corruption, unless he have a mighty intellect, and a firm and generous will.   When these qualifications fail, disturbance, faction, and fighting for the crown is the result. This is the case now, and there is added to it the difficulty of foreign interference in English affairs, both civil and ecclesiastical.   The prince Arthur is the hereditary heir to the crown, but John has a better allegiance, and he has also nationality on his side, so that we are drawn to his party in spite of his selfishness.   But John has not the intellect of Richard III., nor the strength of will to maintain his claim, which, if he had only known it, was the very best he could have had.   He had no faith in such a title, so he is tempted by, and succumbs to the brutal thought of the murder of Arthur; and though he does not actually commit the deed, we can never forgive him the boy's death.

As a hypocrite, King John is but a shadow compared with Richard III.   He is more a hard-hearted coward than a deep, wily, and villainous hypocrite like Richard.   He does not seek his crime and take delight in pursuing it; it is thrust upon him by outward circumstances, and he yields to the temptation.   As Gervinus tells us, "he is not the image of a brutal tyrant, but only the type of a hard nature, without any of the enamel of finer feelings, without any other motives for action than those of the instinct of this same inflexible nature, and of personal interest.   He is severe and earnest, an enemy to cheerfulness and merry laughter, conversant with dark thoughts, of a restless, excited spirit. He is uncommunicative to his best advisers, laconic and reserved."

The scene in which John suggests the murder of Arthur to Hubert, like that between Hubert and Arthur, is one of those masterpieces of Shakspere. Here he shews his hypocrisy; he speaks to Hubert of love, and Hubert professes his affection for the king; he loves him so well that he will do anything for him, though his "death were adjunct to the act." Then, having caught his victim, John says—

> "Hubert throw thine eye
> On yon good boy. I'll tell thee what, my friend,
> He is a very serpent in my way,
> And wheresoe'er this foot of mine doth tread,
> He lies before me. Dost thou understand me?
> Thou art his keeper.
> *Hub.*   And I'll keep him so,
> That he shall not offend your majesty.
> *K. John.* Death.
> *Hub.* My Lord.
> *K. John.* A grave.
> *Hub.* He shall not live.
> *K. John.* Enough.
> I could be merry now. Hubert, I love thee
> Well, I'll not say what I intend for thee."
>   *Act III. iii. 59—71.*

King John moralizes upon the foul deed before his lords, tells us we cannot stand against mortality's strong hand, nor have commandment on the pulse of life. But the lords swear to be revenged, and John's conscience, defiant as it is, gives way.

> "I repent;
> There is no sure foundation set on blood,
> No certain life achieved by others' death."
>   *Act IV. ii. 103—6.*

He seeks to shift the blame of Arthur's death upon Hubert, who, he says, offered such abhorred and fit aspect for the villainy. He shews now the real cowardice of his nature, and exhibits an amount of faint-heartedness and fear that make him contemptible. True, he repented of his sin, but he repented too late; Arthur, the tender object of his fear and hypocrisy, loses his life, and we cannot forgive him the death of the gentle boy.

FALSTAFF.

" Perhaps the most substantial comic character ever invented. Sir John carries a most portly presence in the mind's eye; and in him we behold the 'fulness of the spirit of wit and humour bodily.' "—*Hazlitt, in " Shakespeare's Characters."*

We have now to consider a widely different character, and one far more pleasing, for who is there that does not take delight in jolly old Sir John Falstaff? We feel annoyed that we have to include him in this list of Shakspere's Hypocrites; we are not yet convinced that he is in heart a hypocrite, but others have thought him such, and we must either concur or prove him to be "an honest and true-hearted man!" We feel keenly the difficulty of the position; the character of Falstaff is so complex, his motive so peculiar that we scarcely know how to think of him as he deserves; he himself tells us that it would be "better than a dukedom" to be able to do so, whatever the value of that estimate may be. He appears to us in so many different aspects, and every change reveals something new. He is at once a dupe and a wit; he is both harmless and wicked, cowardly and courageous; a liar without deceit, a knight, a gentleman, and a soldier without either dignity or honour. Surely he must be a consummate hypocrite! But we cannot believe it; we like him too much for that. The business of hypocrisy is to mask *self*, to guard against self-betrayal; the true hypocrite is generally a sly, wily, treacherous fellow, full of ambition—the most inordinate—envy, and malice. He

loves few men, and hates many, especially those who
prosper better than he, for he is extremely selfish, and
delights to elevate himself by pulling others down. But
Falstaff has none of this about him; true he assumes many
similar traits, but he has no malicious intent, he simply
does it to make others laugh; as Hazlitt tells us "he
openly assumes the characters to shew the humorous side of
them: he does it to amuse others as much as to gratify
himself; his unrestrained indulgence in his own appetites
has neither malice nor hypocrisy in it." Our main justification for Falstaff is that he does no great mischief, no evil
consequences follow from his many humorous jokes and
tricks.   He has none of the villany of Richard III., nor
the heartless treachery of Iago: the worst of Falstaff is his
"lie with a good round oath," and his unpaid bills for sack
and sugar, and other refreshment for his "fat sides," owing
to Mrs Quickly.

Gervinus has painted him black enough. He thinks
Falstaff the very personification of the inferior side of man,
and his animal sensual nature.   He is the very embodiment of laziness, epicurean comfort and idleness; selfishness
alone, puts this unwieldy machine in motion.   He is a
robber, a plunderer of the poor, a coward, a braggart, and a
liar. We grant that he appears in all these dresses, and
appears in them to the life, but the dresses are not his own,
he only borrows them for the nonce.   Falstaff could not
live if he was not making fun for somebody, and he assumes
these characters, both to please others and to amuse himself.
We delight in Falstaff so much that he has now become a
typical character, and there are many in the world to be
found, in a greater or less degree, like him.   The writer

had the good fortune, if good fortune it may be called, of living near a faint shadow of Falstaff during a vacation—a big, round-faced, jolly-looking, easy-going fellow. He seldom does any work, unless he can help it, he says it does not agree with him. His good wife provides for him the necessaries of life, and yet she seldom grumbles, for he makes her laugh so much, and everybody else near him, that she would do anything for him, lazy as he is. He, too, believes in the exhilarating influence of "sack," but he never loses his temper, he is always good humoured, and good natured. Despite his faults, those around him will never see him want; they can afford to keep him for the enjoyment they get from his amusing tricks, and his queer and laughable sayings.

Falstaff and his companions have been called "caterpillars of the common-wealth;" they are bound together in a life of idleness and easy living; and the poet has shewn us how such a band is held together, and the kind of attachment existing between them; but if ever roguery and swindling had a chance of being popular, it was when combined with such wit, good humour, and amusement, as that of Falstaff. Laxness and grossness of bodily life and manners could never go so far to assert their independence as when accompanied by such equally sharp intellect and invention. There can be no doubt that Falstaff dislikes work; it disagrees with him; but then he has so much flesh—"more flesh than any other man, and therefore more frailty." He is, in fact, "a tun of man," and nothing but Colossus could bestride him. His *means* are slender, and his *waste* great, which can be taken two ways, but Falstaff says, "I would my *means* were greater, and my *waist* less."

He makes this great bulk of his "the ground tone of his character;" he makes it an excuse for idleness and dissipation; and he affords amusement for others by exaggerating this personal unwieldiness. He shakes his jolly old fat sides with laughter, and "his jokes come upon us with double force and relish from the quantity of flesh through which they make their way." We should not enjoy him half so much were it not for his "portly presence;" we begin to smile to ourselves whenever we think of him—larding the lean earth as he walks along. His jokes are not the dry emanations from a thin, shrivelled wit; they are the outcome of a fine constitution, full of good humour and good nature, overflowing with laughter and good fellowship. He drinks sack to clear his brain, it is to him the soul of his wit, and without sack there is no skill in war, for it "sets the sword a-work."

Falstaff's power is unquestionably in his wit and his intellectual quickness; this is his great redeeming feature, it covers a multitude of his sins. And he has implicit confidence in its power, for if he succeeds in exciting a laugh he feels that he has made a conquest. He is never fast for an answer, and though he be found out in the biggest of lies, he gets out of the difficulty with the greatest ease. He says, "a good wit will make use of anything," and he is not only witty himself, but the cause that wit is in other men; half the wit that seems the Prince's is really his. The rogue blames the young Prince Henry for having corrupted him, and vows "I will be damn'd for never a King's son in Christendom;" but in the next sentence when the Prince suggests taking a purse he responds briskly enough "Where thou wilt lad, I'll make one." His account of the robbery is truly an inimitable scene: how his two men in buckram grew into eleven as the imagination of his own valour increased. He had only escaped by a miracle: eight times thrust through the doublet, four through the hose, his buckler cut through and through, and his sword hacked like a hand-saw. And with what dexterity does he get out of the dilemma when the true story is related? Falstaff had run away, and torn his clothes, and hacked his sword himself; but he says he knew it was the Prince who attacked him, and "was it for him to kill the heir apparent?" So too, in the scene in which he lectures the Prince in the assumed character of the old King, he takes care to give himself a good word, as if he was the most virtuous man in the world. Some have called him a coward, but he is courageous enough to fall asleep behind the arras when officers are in the room ready to charge him with a capital offence. He is searched while asleep; they turn out of his pockets nothing but bills for sack and sugar, yet he swears that there were at least three or four bonds of £40 a piece, and a seal ring of his grandfather's. We may also notice the scene in which he pretends to be deaf to the Chief Justice; and the reconciliation with Mrs Quickly—where he not only settles old debts, but persuades her to sell her plate to lend him £10 more—as instances of his sharpness and quick wit.

He takes delight too in joking with the appearances of others. He says the Prince is a good shallow fellow, and would have made a good pantler, or chipped bread well. He accounts for the Prince's friendship with Poins from the fact that their legs are both of a bigness, or if put in the scales, they would be of the same weight. But when

c

the Prince overhears his abuse Falstaff is quick enough
with a reason. " I despise him before the wicked that the
wicked might not fall in love with him." He compares
Justice Shallow to "a man made after supper of a cheese
paring," and his wit in the recruiting scene, and those with
Shallow and Silence are beyond praise.

Falstaff has a reputation as a soldier, and seems to have
been professed, he was sought out, and got a commission at
the outbreak of the war. Gervinus calls him a coward ;
but surely he was not in truth a coward ! He could fight
if he compelled to do so by circumstances, but he would
much rather " be first in a feast." He asks himself which
will pay best—fighting or running away, and having satisfied himself he acts accordingly. He runs away at
Gadshill because he thinks it safest to run when he is left
single handed to fight two younger, and more active men.
He has recruited for himself a fine company of soldiers, 150
of them, all ragged as Lazarus, with "not a shirt and a half
in all the company." But he thinks them good enough to
toss, for they'll fill a pit as well as better men. He leads
them into the part of the field where they will get well
peppered, and withdraws himself to a quiet place to breath
a while, where he finds time to rest, and to refresh himself
with a bottle of sack, just within reach of a battle which
disposes of the lives of princes. His soliloquy on Honour
is characteristic. He fully believes that his honour pricks
him on to the fight, but he cannot convince himself that the
same honour will set on a leg or an arm, or even take away
the grief of a wound : so he will have none of it. He
shows that discretion is the better part of his valour, in
his fight with Douglas, when he falls down after two or

three passes of the sword, and by the act saves his life. He reaches the height of his ingenuity when he claims to have killed Hotspur, and in the taking of Coleville in the second part. This must be " booked with the rest of the valourous deeds of the day."

Very just indignation has been expressed at the Prince's treatment of Falstaff. He has relied throughout upon the Prince rewarding him on his attaining the crown; but at the coronation the Prince does not know Falstaff. Lloyd excuses his conduct by saying that this was the first public act of the Prince, and it must form the turning point in his history; he must display something more than ordinary self-command. This may be true, but we cannot forgive the Prince his heartless conduct in ordering Falstaff's banishment : the least he could have done would have been to provide for the last days of one who had afforded him so much harmless amusement and pleasure. What becomes of Falstaff we know not, but we are assured that we could " better have spared a better man."

PAROLLES.

"A most notable coward, an infinite and endless liar, an hourly promise b   ker, the owner of no good quality."

Act III. vi 9—12.

PAROLLES.

"All's well that ends well" is one of Shakspere's most pleasant comedies; but the humour here is of a more serious nature. Parolles has some of Falstaff's qualities, but they are of the worst kind. He has all the bragging and the lying of Falstaff, and he is a bigger coward; but he has none of Sir John's sparkling wit, none of his good fellowship and good humour; there is no trait in his character which reconciles us to him. We can tolerate Falstaff, with all his faults, but Parolles has not one redeeming feature.

Like Falstaff, he is the hanger-on to a prince—the parasite of Bertram, Count of Rousillon, who is young and handsome, but careless, and with little insight into human character; he allows himself to be led too much by this shallow clown, whose very name suggests that he has no stability in him. Lafeu, the ancient Lord, who has more experience than the Prince, makes a true estimate of Parolles; he had thought him at one time to be a pretty wise fellow, but the more he saw of him the more he disliked him, and soon became convinced that he was a vessel of no great burden:

"You are more saucy with Lords and honourable personages than the commission of your birth and virtue gives you heraldry. You are not worth another word else I'd call you Knave."

He has been called a counterfoil of Helena—one of the sweetest of our poet's creations—who is in love with

Bertram, but the Count disregards her, he says he hates her, and his heartlessness is encouraged by this unprincipled knave Parolles. He persuades Bertram to leave the country, and join the wars in France; it is cowardly and boyish, he says, to spend his days at home, it is simply putting his "honour in a box." They go to Florence, where Parolles' bragging pretensions to bravery are put to test, and he is found wanting. The episode of "bringing off the drum" is almost as amusing as the robbery scene with Falstaff. He is sent on this mission at the suggestion of the lords, who wish to expose the coward to the young Count, for they are well assured that he will return with some invention with "two or three probable lies clapp'd upon it." Parolles goes on his mission, and is closely followed by one of the lords and some soldiers; he appears on the battle-field—but not far from his own camp—at ten o'clock, two hours before the appointed time for his return. He comes, however, not to find his drum, but rather to find out

"What shall I say I have done?"

for it must be some plausible invention. He feels that of late his beguiling artifices have not succeeded as they were wont, and disgraces have knocked too often at his door; he has been too foolhardy with his tongue—talked much and done little, so he will redeem himself by a monster invention. He thinks he will give himself some hurts, and say he got them in exploit, yet he is too cowardly for this, it will pain him too much ; he would like the cutting of his garments, the baring of his beard, or the breaking of his sword, to serve the same purpose ; or to drown his clothes and say he was stripped of them. But in the midst of this useless reasoning he is seized by the sham enemy, who have heard it all, and he is blind-folded. Then how the coward pleads for his life!—for he loves himself most dearly—he will do anything, disclose all the affairs of his camp, tell the number of their forces, if he may only live. They put him in the stocks all night, and in the morning they take him before one whom he supposes to be the general of the enemy, in reality his own Count Bertram. Then what a fool he makes of himself ; what a hypocrite and what a coward he proves himself to be ! He betrays all the secrets of his camp, and blackballs the Count and the officers. Duke Dumain is everything that is bad, the Count nothing but a foolish, dangerous, and lascivious boy. When he is unmuffled, he is rather surprised, but he soon gets over it—

> "Yet am I thankful: if my heart were great
> 'T would burst at this. Captain I'll be no more ;
> But I will eat and drink, and sleep as soft
> As captain shall: simply the thing I am
> Shall make me live. Who knows himself a braggart,
> Let him fear this ; for it will come to pass,
> That every braggart shall be found an ass.
> Rust, sword ! cool, blushes ! and Parolles, live !
> Safest in shame ! being fool'd, by foolery thrive !
> There 's place and means for every man alive !"
>
> *Act IV. iii. 338—357.*

What becomes of him, we do not know, nor do we care, for he has nothing about him that would make us interested in his future.

CLAUDIUS, KING OF DENMARK.

> "Like a mildew'd ear,
> Blasting his wholesome brother."
>
> *Hamlet, Act III.*, iv. 65—6.

> "Thus was I, sleeping, by a brother's hand,
> Of life, of crown, of queen, at once despatched :
> Cut off even in the blossoms of my sin,
> No reckoning made, and sent to my account
> With all my imperfections on my head :
> O, horrible! O, horrible! most horrible!
>
> *The Ghost, Act I. v.* 74—80.

CLAUDIUS, KING OF DENMARK.

Our poet is now in the third period of his dramatic writings, and "Hamlet" represents his entrance to his series of great tragic productions. He is now beginning to sound the depths of the human heart, to study the great mystery of life, and man's tendency to evil; for crime is no longer a small thing with him; it is not now as in his youth, when he looked at sin with some indifference, when he passed over faults with a light heart, and judged crime with an easy verdict. Henceforth the "universe of the law" must prevail; if the law be broken, the offender must suffer to the utmost extent. It has been said that in this period the poet judges too harshly, for he lets his characters bring about their own destruction, without giving them warning of the approaching danger—"man lives in a world where he is his own providence."

So much has been said about Hamlet that we have no need to add anything to it. His story is well known—how his father has been murdered by his uncle, now married to his mother, and thus snatched the crown from him, the sole heir; we have only to deal in a few words with this

villain of an uncle, this traitor who robbed Denmark of its
wisest king—of a

> "Combination and form indeed
> Where every god did seem to set his seal
> To give the world the assurance of a man."

After the King has committed the murder, with feigned
affection he pretends to console Hamlet on his loss.   He
says it is commendable, a sweet thing, in Hamlet, to be
sorrowful for his father, but to persevere in obstinate
condolement is contrary to the will of Heaven.   He prays
Hamlet to think of him as a father, for he bears towards
him the dearest love possible for a father to a son.   But
how can Hamlet love him—he, who has murdered his
father, he, who has married his mother but two months
after!   Hamlet is visited by his dead father's spirit, and
urged to take his revenge; but Hamlet is a man of thought
and meditation, not of action; so he delays, he can see no
justice in committing a sin for which he condemns another.
He reasons with himself, and then devises a play to
ascertain the real guilt of Claudius, and his guilt is
established beyond a doubt, for no sooner does the actor
Lucanius pour the rank mixture into the sleeper's ear than
the King starts up, his perjured soul smiting him, and he
hastens from the place.   When the King is alone he feels
the weight of his sin—

> Oh! my offence is rank, it smells to heaven."

The hypocrite would fain look up and pray; but what form
of prayer would serve him?   How can he be forgiven for
so foul a murder—the murder of a brother!   Hamlet finds
him upon his knees; now he thinks he might venture to
have his revenge, and thus send his soul to heaven; but he

hesitates again, he thinks this no revenge, he will wait a while; he will catch the King in some of his viler acts, and then despatch him. The King thus finds his foe in Hamlet, and he wants to send him to a bloody death in England; finally, he leads Hamlet into the trap of playing swords with Laertes with poisoned weapons. But, after all, there is in Hamlet a terrible reserve power—a power of desperate and sudden action; and in the last scene, with a final effort, with a strength which leaps up before it is finally extinguished, he accomplishes the revenge of his murdered father, and the punishment of the vile murderer.

ANGELO.

Shame to him, whose cruel striking
Kills for faults of his own liking;
Twice treble shame on Angelo,
To weed my vice, and let his grow.
Oh! what may man within him hide,
Though angel on the outward side!"

Duke, Act III. ii. 269—274.

ANGELO.

In "measure for measure" the predominant idea of the "universe of law" is more clearly marked. Shakspere preaches here his doctrine of "an eye for an eye, a tooth for a tooth," "an Angelo for a Claudio, death for death." Weakness yielding to temptation must be punished to the utmost.

The play is full of genius, and wise and deep sayings, but it is a very repulsive one; we cannot take a deep interest in it, nor feel pleased, the subject is so unattractive. As W. Watkiss Lloyd says, "We never throughout the play get into the free, open, joyous atmosphere, so invigorating in other works of Shakspere; the oppressive gloom of the prison, the foul breath of the brothel, are only exchanged for the chilly damp of conventual walls, or the oppressive retirement of the monastery." Its pictures are disgusting and contemptible, not only for its sin, but for its hypocrisy ; we have dissoluteness on one side, with religious austerity on the other; pride and unblushing vice contrasted with a great show of ostentatious virtue.

The scene is Vienna, which is represented as the very centre of sensual defilement and moral corruption; here it "boils and bubbles till it o'er-runs." All virtue and decorum has been lost; in the streets we meet only wayward and dissolute men and women, with a desire for nothing but wickedness and self-indulgence. Debauchery is the common custom, it has become the talk and daily business of life. This miserable state of things is the result of neglect in carrying out the laws; they have been for fourteen years entirely suspended. They are severe enough and sufficient to check the crime, but the reigning Duke has been too kind-hearted, too full of the "milk of human kindness" to apply them. They have been laid aside and allowed to slumber; things have come to such a pitch that some-thing must be done. But the Duke cannot do it himself; it is too much for his "innate mildness," so he resolves to withdraw from the scene and appoint a deputy. Angelo is the man chosen for this office, for, as Escalus say—

> "If any man in Vienna be of worth
> To undergo such ample grace and honour,
> It is Lord Angelo."

He is a man of strict and firm abstinence; he is precise, stands on his guard with envy—scarcely confesses that his blood flows, or that "his appetite is more to bread than to stone." Lucio says that his blood is very "snow-broth"—a "man who never felt the wanton stings and motions of the senses." This is the man whom the Duke selects as his deputy, and at first sight he seems to be most suitable for the office: just the man to bring the city back to a state of happiness, purity, and virtue—to put down a sin which seems to be so much at variance with the character of the deputy. He is a man of ability, well versed in politics and law, and in the study of these weighty subjects, he seems to have suppressed all feelings of affection; he has formed or himself severe principles of moral conduct, and has laughed at the foolish devotion of love in others. He is

ambitious too, as most hypocrites are, and he makes his
seeming virtue an instrument to his ambition; he aspires to
be powerful, to outward rank and dignity, and to attain his
object, he must never for a moment forget his hitherto
reputation of virtue.

But Angelo's meanness is revealed at the very outset.
The Duke knew that the Deputy had been betrothed to
Marianna, sister to Frederick, a famous naval hero. But
the brother had perished, and her dowry had gone to the
bottom of the sea with him: so Angelo forsakes her.
Without money she is of no use to him, and he seeks to
cover his heartlessness by pretended discoveries against her
virtue and honour; to colour his proceedings by the
basest insinuations against her chastity. The Duke has,
therefore, determined to test Angelo's strength of character—
how he will be affected in a wider sphere of action—how
this precise and severely moral man will conduct himself
when brought in contact with evil and temptation. He
disguises himself as a friar, pretending that he is going on
a journey, and retires to watch the course of events as
it developes around him.

The official career of Angelo now begins. He hunts up
all the corrupt houses, and orders them to be plucked down.
He fills his prisons with offensive criminals of all sorts; all
the lower mischiefs and abuses are rooted out; the
constabulary, hitherto appointed indifferently, is corrected
once for all. Angelo has no mercy, his character is most
inflexible; whatever else is left undone, these wrong doers
must be severely punished, the dignity of the law must be
upheld. This man, who prides himself on his virtue, takes
a delight in intimidating others; he is ambitious, and his

great desire is to make himself a name, to have power, and to govern. This trait in his character leads him to treat all classes alike—to deal out justice impartially, without respect of persons; so he is not content with bringing up the loose vagabonds of the street, he flies at higher game, and must needs arrest a young nobleman, Claudio, whom he publicly leads to prison, to the scandal of the whole town, for the sake of one single offence. He and Julietta have been guilty of this severely denounced frailty, but surely in its most venial form, for the lovers are still faithful to each other, they are united by all the bonds except the outward ceremony. Yet Claudio is adjudged by Angelo to die. Escalus intercedes with the Deputy for the young nobleman ; he is conscious of the recent laxness of the law, and of man's proneness to evil. He suggests to Angelo the possibility that even he may fall a victim to the same crime. Angelo replies almost with a sneer, and with implicit confidence in his own virtue—

> " It is one thing to be tempted, Escalus,
> Another thing to fall   *   *   *
> *   *   But rather tell me
> When I that censure him do so offend,
> Let my own judgment pattern out my death,
> And nothing come in partial."

He little knew how soon he was to have this very judgment brought upon him ; he little knew that he, who had prided himself that sensual delight had never stirred his feelings— "when men were fond, he had smiled as at a contemptible and incredible thing"—was to fall a victim to that very passion which he so much ridiculed. But this feeling of virtue in Angelo is exaggerated, it is all outward show ; he lays greater stress upon the outward appearance of virtue than upon the inward reality.

Claudio has a sister, Isabella, a novice of the sisterhood of Saint Clare ; she is beautiful and accomplished, and has many intellectual qualities, and mental endowments. And Claudio sends a request to his sister that she go and petition Angelo for his life. He knows that she has many persuasive powers, that "she will play with reason in discourse." Isabella visits Angelo, and now the real character of this would-be saint reveals itself. He is inflamed with lust at the sight of the beautiful maiden ; he has never before been exposed to such temptation ; he has always laughed at it, and gone his way rejoicing in his own strength. But now his conduct at the very sight of the maiden, and his "come again to-morrow," reveal the hold that the temptation has upon him. When alone he wonders at his own weakness—how he that has professed himself a saint could be so tempted by a saint ; but he has entered upon the road to his ruin, he cannot stifle his passion, he can think of nothing but his desire for Isabel. Even his prayers are a mockery—

> "Heaven hath my empty words,
> Whilst my invention, hearing not my tongue,
> Anchors on Isabel."

On the morrow Isabel visits Angelo again, and repeats her request. Angelo is now fully given up to his desires, and he makes his base proposal to allow the ransom of her brother if she will submit to his desires. She understands him perfectly, but thinks he is perhaps only testing her virtue ; she comments upon the frailty of her sex, and then he speaks with more confidence, and urges his demand. With what hypocrisy does this tongue of his, which has so often uttered the sentence of death against this abominable sin, invite the maiden to a far more disgraceful perpetration of the same sin ! Through the management of the Duke, however, his vile purpose is frustrated, though he himself thinks he has effected it, and the forsaken Marianna takes the place of Isabel. Angelo has now reached the length of his crime, and remorse seizes him. He feels keenly the dishonour which will now be placed upon him. This precise man, this would-be model of virtue, is proved to be nothing but "an outward-sainted deputy;" he is floored upon his own ground, upon the very trait in his character he was most proud of; such is his downfall that the "very body and soul of his digrity and honour are lacerated at the same moment."

The Duke saves the life of Claudio, which Angelo would have so ruthlessly sacrificed. In the sham scene of the last act the hypocrisy of Angelo is publicly exposed. The sneak feels his position bitterly, he knows not where to hide his face before the now undisguised Duke. He cannot conceal his guilt, he is "guiltier than the guiltiness ;" he begs for nothing but "immediate sentence and sequent death." But Isabel pleads for him, "since his act did not o'ertake his bad intent," and the hypocrite is forgiven on the condition that he at once marry Marianna. It was not likely that the Duke could sentence to death Angelo, who had been tempted, and had given way to the temptation, in the prosecution of a work which he himself did not feel equal to; a temptation which had been laid upon him by the revival of that severe discipline which had been for so many years neglected.

IAGO.

" Oh ! Sparton dog !
More fell than anguish, hunger, or the sea !
Look on the tragic loading of this bed ;
This is thy work : the object poison's sight.
Let it be hid."

Ladovico, Act V. ii. 303—307.

IAGO.

In cruel and wicked invention, and in heartless treachery, Iago stands second to none amongst Shakspere's hypocrites; and he is one of the most powerful of our poet's inventions— "one of the supererogations of his genius." Iago has the two-fold quality of being both repulsive and attractive, for while we are incensed at his extreme wickedness, we are interested in the skilful means he adopts to gain his ends. He is indeed a genius, gifted with great mental vigour and a penetrating intellect. He is a great observer of men and manners; he looks deep down into men's characters, into their springs of action, with a far-seeing eye, and he knows exactly how to use every one of them to suit his own purpose. He never seems to be embarassed; he spreads his nets with such skill that no one can escape. He brings every one near him, within his grip, and like a ruling despot makes them serve him; he thinks the men and women around him mere puppets to dance to his fiddling. Roderigo is simply a machine to do as he is told, though needing at times a little persuasion ; Othello—poor deluded Othello—is to him "an ass to be led by the nose;" consciencious Cassio a "mere moraller ;" the pure and faithful Desdemona, a poor and worthless thing. As Hazlitt very forcibly puts it—"he gets up an amateur tragedy in real life, but instead of employing his invention upon imaginary

characters, he gets up a plot at home, casts the principal
parts amongst his friends and connections, and rehearses it
in a downright good earnest, with steady nerves and
unabated resolution." Iago is one of those dangerously
endowed beings whose brains have become sharp and
inventive with the hardening of their hearts. He plots the
ruin of his friends as an exercise of his ingenuity; his
gaiety arises from the success of his treachery, and his ease
from the torture he inflicts upon others.

He is an absolute infidel, a confirmed sceptic with regard
to all that is pure and good and noble; moral beauty is a
quality unknown to him. He thinks it quite consistent to
live in a world in which all men are knaves and fools, and
everything that is beautiful and noble "a gross element of
the earth." There is no such thing as virtue, it is "a fig"
to him; and reputation, even this is an indifferent thing.
He talks of it nicely enough to Othello, and bursts into a
fit of passion at the expression of doubt of his sincerity;
but to Cassio he says that reputation is an idle and most
false imposition, got without merit, and lost without
deserving. There is much more sense in having received
material harm than in having lost one's reputation. Iago
is something of a philosopher, too, and has been compared
to Hamlet in his turn of mind. But how strikingly
different are they in character! While Hamlet is free from
everything that is mean and villainous, Iago is free from
everything that is great and noble. In his soliloquies, what
fiendish delight he takes in the contemplation of his own
hideous plans? He revels in the thought that his nefarious
schemes are progressing towards a successful end. He
regards it as a triumph of his intellect that he has almost

equalled the demons of darkness in the ingenuity of his
devices. Nay, he surpasses the arch-fiend himself, for he,
in the contemplation of disturbing the unsullied happiness
of our first parents, had *some* pricks of conscience.

> "And should I at your harmless innocence
> Melt, as I do, yet public reason just,
> Honour and empire with revenge enlarged,
> By conquering this new world, compels me now
> To do, what else, though damn'd, I should abhor."
>
> *Milton, Paradise Lost, Book IV.*

But Iago has no such compunctions; he rather derives
pleasure from the thought that he has power to mar such
happiness.

> "Oh! you are well tuned now;
> But I will set down the keys that make the music
> As honest as I am."

And he has such assurance in his plans that every time he
undermines their peace he appears to be their best friend
and their most faithful adviser; he always contrives to
clothe his malicious lies with a semblance of truth. The
difficult thing to understand in Iago is to find a motive
sufficient for the display of so much villainy and hypocrisy.
Some have called the character altogether un-natural because
they have failed to find it. But his motive is undoubtedly
one of the love of power—"an insatiable craving for action
of the most difficult and dangerous kind," coupled with an
unquenchable desire for revenge on being slighted. To
form, therefore, a true estimate of this character we must
consider in detail his connection with the characters around
him in the play.

He has engendered a bitter hatred against Cassio for having
obtained the lieutenancy to Othello over his head. At once
he fixes his mind upon Cassio's ruin and gaining the office

for himself.   He cannot brook the thought that he has been more lightly estimated than the "great arithmetician," as he contemptuously calls Cassio—

> "A man that never set a squadron in the field,
> Nor the division of a battle knows,
> More than a spinster."

Still he feels Cassio's superiority in manners, for "there is a dull beauty in his life that makes me ugly."   With what cunning he succeeds in making Cassio drunk, excites Roderigo against him, and brings him into such disfavour with the Moor that the lieutenant is dismissed !   And then he has the impudence to tell Othello—

> "I had rather have this tongue cut from my mouth
> Than it should do offence to Michael Cassio;
> Yet, I persuade myself, to speak the truth
> Shall nothing wrong him."

He expressed his sympathy with Cassio, and moralizes upon the worthlessness of reputation.   But he is not satisfied yet.   Having succeeded thus far, he forms new plans Cassio, thus disgraced, must now be an instrument to incite a feeling of jealousy in the breast of the Moor.   He, therefore, counsels Cassio to solicit Desdemona to intercede for him.   Here his opinion of the fair lady is exactly the opposite of that expressed to Roderigo—"she is of so free, so kind, so apt, so blessed disposition that she holds it a vice in her goodness not to do more than she is requested."   And what is he then that says Iago is a villain ?   Surely this is the very best advice he could give Cassio.   But his good advice is accompanied by the resolve—

> "Whiles this honest fellow
> Plies Desdemona to repair his fortunes,
> And she for him pleads strongly to the Moor,
> I will pour this pestilence into his ear,
> That she repeals him for her body's lust;

And by how much she strives to do him good,
She shall undo her credit with the Moor.
So will I turn her virtue into pitch,
And out of her own goodness make a net
That shall enmesh them all."

II. iii. 350—354.

He has yet two things to do, he says: first, his wife must get Cassio and Desdemona together, while he will bring the Moor to see the interview. This done, Cassio will be best out of the way, so he excites Roderigo against him, sees Cassio wound him, and then by giving Cassio a thrust, he removes both at one stroke, and after he has done it, seeks to lay all the blame on Bianca.

Roderigo is perhaps the greatest tool in the hands of Iago; like Othello, he is completely duped by the villain, but while Othello never doubts his sincerity, Roderigo is repeatedly suspicious that he is being cheated, and he is as often overcome by the subtle arguments of Iago. If he cannot gain attention any other way, he turns moralist :

"Our bodies are as gardens to the which our wills are gardeners; so that if we will plant nettles, or sow lettuce ; set hyssop and weed up thyme; supply it with one gender of herbs, or distract it with many; either to have it sterile with idleness, or manured with industry ; why, the power and corrigible authority in this lies in our wills."—*Act I. iii. 321—333.*

He scoffs at Roderigo for thinking to drown himself ; laughs at his qualms of conscience, and bids him put money in his purse. He gains the victory, and succeeds in getting Roderigo to watch Cassio, so as to find some fault with him, "to provoke his sudden choler" and then to strike him. His plan is again successful. In the fourth act Roderigo begins again to be dissatisfied. He has found that the words and the performances of Iago are in no way akin. He has wasted his means, and received none of Iago's promised rewards for the jewels lent as presents to Desdemona. But Iago entangles him in another plot, and this time the inhuman dog succeeds in bringing about the end of the too devoted Roderigo.

There is, perhaps, no greater contrast in all the main figures of Shakspere than between Othello and Iago. The former has been compared to the lion of the desert, but the latter, "assuredly some malignant power that lurks in the eye, and that fills with venom the fang of the serpent, would seem to have brought *him* into existence." Both are possessed with a feeling of jealousy, but compared with Othello's, the jealousy of Iago is only artificial, it is merely the means to other ends—his revenge on the Moor. The ruling thought in Othello's mind is to destroy his wife; the ruling thought in Iago's is to destroy the suspected paramour.

As we have seen, the Moor has preferred Cassio to Iago for the lieutenancy, and this has awakened Iago's bitter hatred. Gervinus very justly finds fault with Othello for this preferment of "the bookish theoric" to Iago, whose bravery and excellent soldierly qualities are unquestioned. Othello should have thought twice before he had acted thus towards Iago, who, once excited, filled all his soul with schemes of revenge. But to the unsuspecting Moor, all this was unknown. Iago was to him a man of honesty and trust, and he little thought that his action would bring about such painful results. Iago resolves at once that he will be revenged; henceforth he will follow the Moor only "to serve his turn upon him." He says there are some servants who wear out their time like their master's ass, "for nought but provender." There are others, trimmed in the forms and visages of duty, who

> "Keep yet their hearts attending on themselves,
> And throwing but shows of service on their lords,
> Do well thrive by them."

Such a soul as this he professes himself to be, and here he gives us the key-note of his hypocrisy, resolving in future to wear his heart upon his sleeve for "daws to peck at." He is not long before he gets to work—for this play is the swiftest in action in all Shakspere—and his first act is to incite Brabantio against the Moor, and to disturb the first hour the married couple spent together. In the next scene he is the apparent friend of Othello, as opposed to Brabantio. He pretends to "show out a flag and sign of love" towards the Moor, who trusts him so much as to assign to him the conveyance of his fair wife (Desdemona) on the journey across the sea. At the close of Act I. he reveals the first thoughts of his evil scheme ; as yet it is a mere bubble, it floats but dimly in his mind, but it afterwards grows to proportions which he himself would scarcely have dreamed of.

"I hate the Moor ;

He holds me well ;
The better shall my purpose work on him.
Cassio's a proper man : let me see now ;
To get his place, and to plume up my will,
In double knavery,—How, how?—Let's see :-
After some time to abuse Othello's ear,
That he is too familiar with his wife ;
He hath a person, and a smooth dispose,
To be suspected : fram'd to make women false.
The Moor is of a free and open nature,
That thinks men honest that but seem to be so,
And will as tenderly be led by the nose
As asses are,—
I have 't ;—it is engendered :—hell and night
Must bring this monstrous birth to the world's light."

Act II. iii. 300—404.

At the close of Act II. his plan has assumed a more definite shape, and in Act III.—which Furnival thinks the most powerful in all the plays—he sets himself to the work of arousing the feeling of deep jealousy in the breast of the

E

Moor. Here his hypocritical arts display their most masterly power; nothing ever equalled the profound dissimulation and the dexterous artifice displayed in this dialogue. He stops and brooks the deep workings of treachery under the mask of love and interest, anxious watchfulness, and cool earnestness. There is "a passion of hypocrisy," as Hazlitt puts it, marked in every line. He instills drop by drop, the subtle and deadly poison into the soul of Othello; with diabolical ingenuity he feeds the jealous flame he has kindled in the breast of the Moor, and that, too, without making any direct statement. He simply suggests in a hesitating manner, half expressing, half repressing, that the Moor has need to beware of jealousy, that "green-eye'd monster which doth make the meat it feeds on," and then he turns the suspicion on Cassio, and bids Othello guard well his wife.

After this victory Iago's task is an easy one. He devises the scheme of the handkerchief :

> "For trifles light as air are to the jealous
> Forms strong as proofs of Holy writ."

When the two meet again Othello wants further proof of his wife's unfaithfulness, and expresses a doubt as to "honest" Iago's sincerity. At this the villain adds a finishing touch to his hypocrisy by that almost inconceivable outburst of pretended rage :

> "O grace ! O Heaven forgive me !
> Are you a man? have you a soul, or sense ?—
> God bu wi' you; take mine office.— O wretched fool,
> That liv'st to make thine honesty a vice !—
> O monstrous world ! Take note, take note, O world !
> To be direct and honest is not safe.—
> I thank you for this profit ; and, from hence,
> I'll love no friend sith love breeds such offence."
>
> *Act III. iii. 375—381.*

But Iago is by no means bewildered : he will give Othello further proof. He entangles the Moor in another delusion, and poisons his mind with the revolting images of Cassio's dream. He touches the weakest thread in the Moor's nature, and fills his mind with thoughts that never subsequently lose their hold upon him. Then follows the interview between Othello and Desdemona ; and as soon as Iago hears that they have parted in anger he hastens to the Moor in triumph to ply again his wicked arts. But it is too much for Othello ; he falls in a swoon, and with what brutal coldness Iago sees it all, and glories in the success of his schemes,—

> " Work on.
> My medicine work ! Thus credulous fools are caught ;
> And many worthy and chaste dames, even thus,
> All guiltless, meet reproach."
>
> *Act IV. i. 44—47.*

Iago's work with Othello is now complete. He has so firmly planted the feeling of jealousy in his breast that nothing can erase it—not even the heart-rending pleadings of the beautiful and innocent Desdemona. The Moor entertains all the doubts possible against his wife, but not the slightest doubt of Iago's honesty ever crosses his mind, and we are pained to see Iago's wicked plans succeed, and the lives of the innocent sacrificed.

We could forgive Iago his sin against Othello, and Cassio, and Roderigo, but of his sin against Desdemona, we could never forgive him. With what pitiless insensibility, with what brutal indifference does he see her fall a victim to his malignity ? The depth of his wickedness is manifested towards *her*, for she has done him no wrong, she has excluded him from no office or higher rank. He must,

therefore, direct himself to her inward perfection, to her
chastity, and the beauty of her character :

> " A maiden never bold ;
> Of spirit so still and quiet, that her motion
> Blushed at herself."

But he tries to make himself believe that her virtue and
goodness are mere mockery.   Roderigo thinks her "full of
the most blessed condition."   Iago thinks her no better
than other people, that she too must understand the art of
deceiving, that sensuality and fickleness belong to her as
well as to others.   He seems to take a delight in finding out
the worst side of everybody, and to prove himself an over-
match for all.   If he finds no evil he will devise means to
make believe there is some.   The hypocrite disguises his
opinions from Desdemona by relating "old paradoxes."
He declares himself a slanderer, and proves it by
characterising different women, and praising the worst best.
His reply to her demand as to what he would bestow upon
the most deserving woman is, indeed, a masterpiece of
satire : it has "light without warmth, clearness without
feeling,"—and he declares her most truly deserving good
to enough "suckle fools and chronicle small beer."
We have thus traced the development of this hateful
character : how he has grown in wickedness, depth after
depth of his sinful depravity disclosed.   We stand aghast
at the contemplation of him, and were he not a creation of
Shakspere's we could scarcely believe him to be human.
To think that a man who has only looked upon this world
for four-times seven years, should be so destitute of the " milk
of human kindness'" and all the better impulses of human
nature !   But Iago has an inherent proneness to evil, and

this is accompanied by a great and brilliant intellect. Were it not for this—for his indefatigable industry and inexhaustible resources, which divert our attention from the wicked end he has in view—the character could never be tolerated.

Of Iago's end we know nothing ; he himself asks us—

" Demand from me nothing; what you know, you know
From this time forth, I never will speak word."

The triumph of vice is of short duration—*" magna est veritas et praecalebit,"* and though the lives of Desdemona and Othello are sacrificed to the cowardly vengeance of Iago, their virtue and honour are more valued than their lives. We admire too the devoted fidelity of Æmilia—the wife of Iago—when she perceives her husband's guilt, and we participate in the hope—

" But for this slave Iago,
If there be any cunning cruelty
That can torment him much, and hold him long
It shall be so."

THE HYPOCRITES IN "KING LEAR."

" KING LEAR is the greatest single achievement in the poetry of the Teutonic or Northern genius."—*Dowden.*

We now come to the study of the hyprocrites in *King Lear* : to the story of the passionate King and the ingratitude of his daughters ; and the story of the deluded Earl and the ingratitude and treachery of his bastard son. We are now in Shakspere's sorrowful period—" in the depths "—the period when he is sounding the very foundations of the human heart, and the great mysteries of life. In *King Lear* the poet found a subject giving full scope to his power of representing unrestrained nature. He has here pictured a society in which every man's hand seems lifted against his fellow, where even the powerful restraint of the family tie has no hold whatever upon men and women ; the dearest and most sacred bonds are disregarded, and unrestrained passion in full sway.

The play is one of Shakspere's greatest achievements. Hazlitt gives it first place amongst the poet's works, for it is the one in which he is most in earnest. *Othello* touches the heart of Furnival more, yet he places it amongst the first three of the poet's greatest works, while Dowden thinks it " the greatest achievement in the poetry of the Teutonic or Northern genius. In its largeness of conception and the variety of its details, in its grotesqueness and sublimity, it owns kinship with the great cathedrals of gothic architecture." It has been compared to a tempest in which everything is in motion, with Lear, like a great unmanageable vessel tossed about by its fury ; a victim to his unrestrained passion he is lashed about in all directions by the unmerciful waves—stripped first of his affection, then of power ; then of home and shelter, last of reason ; and finally learning the preciousness of true love at the moment when it must for ever be renounced.

GONERIL AND REGAN.

"Gorgons rather than women : monsters of ingratitude."—Dowden.

"They are thoroughly hateful."—Hazlitt.

The story of King Lear and the ingratitude of his two daughters is well known. The first words of the play lead us to believe that the kingdom has been divided into three parts—two equal parts for his elder daughters, Goneril and Regan, and a third more opulent portion for his youngest and favourite daughter Cordelia. But the King is eccentric and very passionate, he has ever "but slenderly known himself," and his love of flattery demands some test of the affection of his daughters ; they must make a public confession of it before they receive the dowry—as if he would bribe them into a false avowal of their love, a temptation to which two of them yield. The three daughters are called before him. Goneril, the first born, in answer to the question of the extent of her love, pleads

that she loves her father more than words can express—
" dearer than eyesight, space, and liberty . . . no less
than life." Regan wishes to be valued at the same price as
her sister, only Goneril has come too short, for she finds her
highest joys, joys which the most sensitive part of her
nature is capable of possessing, in the love of her father.
But Cordelia, the young and beautiful Cordelia, the joy and
the happiness of her aged father, the one he loved most,
what is her answer?—Simply " nothing ! " She is so
conscious of her love, and so disgusted with the false
pretensions of her sisters that she will answer—" nothing ! "
With indiscreet simplicity she tells her father the truth of
her love, that she loved him according to her bond, as a
child to a father—no more, no less. Then the impetuous
and ungoverned nature of Lear bursts forth in all its fury.
He divides Cordelia's portion between the other sisters,
banishes the faithful Kent for trying to show the King his
injustice, disclaims Cordelia, and gives her to France with a
curse as her dowry. But Cordelia knows what hypocrites
her sisters are, and would scorn to have professed as they
had done, a love she did not feel. With a sorrowful heart
she commits her father to their care, though she would
gladly leave him in a better place, and bids them use him
well. Their hypocrisy is revealed in the first words they
utter—"prescribe us not our duties"—conscience pricks
them on being thus reminded of their duty ; naturally they
hate such advice, having laid their wicked plans, having
determined to do wrong, and made hypocritical pretensions
to do the right. Cordelia leaves them with many misgivings
for the safety and welfare of her father. But time will
prove her devotedness and the truthfulness of her affection ;

it will unfold, too, the "plaited cunning" of her wicked
sisters, for—

"Who cover faults at last shame them derides."

It is arranged that Lear shall stay with his two daughters
alternately month by month, with Goneril first. But no
sooner does the King get there than she begins to be
disrespectful towards him, and to find all manner of fault.
The sisters have mutually arranged that he shall no longer
be his own master; he has given away his power, and must
no longer have a will of his own, or, as the fool puts it,
since he has "made his daughters his mother"* he must
suffer himself to be treated as a child. The King has not
been with Goneril a fortnight before she proposes to rob
him of the hundred followers he has reserved for himself—
"a little to disquantity his train." Now Lear begins to
feel his true position—how woeful indeed it is! He perceives the ingratitude—that marble-hearted fiend—of this
his love-professing daughter. How he repents his haste
with Cordelia! how he has magnified her simple sin in his
heart! He will stay no longer with Goneril. He has yet
another daughter, who, he is sure, will be kind and comforting to him, and he will at once go to her. The heartless
Goneril lets him go, having received the curse of her aged
father, and she laughs in her sleeve at his foolishness. The
sisters have arranged how to treat the old man; he is to
have no peace and no happiness while near them; they
know his infirmity and his waywardness, they are sure he
will give them some trouble, they must, therefore, act at

* Compare Essay on Shakspere's Clowns—third period. King
Lear's Fool.

once—"I' the heat"—for they will never be content until
he is out of the way.

The unhappy Lear goes to Regan now, but, alas! for him,
she is too much like her sister—as like her as "a crab is to
a crab." Regan tells him she cannot believe that her sister
would be so unkind, reminds him of his age and infirmity,
and asks him to go back to Goneril, to be ruled and led by
a discretion that knows him better than he knows himself.
Poor Lear! he is bewildered, dumfounded—he who has
been so powerful, so high-minded, so dignified, and com-
manding, reduced to such a state of dependence! He
cannot, and will not go back to Goneril; he is so dejected,
brought so low, that he even goes on his knees and begs
that Regan will give him "raiment, bed, and food." But
Regan, too, has become so hardened, she has listened so
much to the evil suggestions of her sister that she cannot
be moved; she, too, denies him residence, she pleads that
her house is too small to receive the old man—in fact, any
excuse to get rid of him.

Lear leaves his daughters in despair, they have turned
him out of doors, he may go where he will. What a
pitiful and heart-rending picture is that of the old man in
the storm: such a night—rain, thunder, wind, and fire.
But these are as nothing compared with the unkindness of
his daughters; he can endure the storm, but the ingratitude
of his daughters, Oh! 'tis foul, 'tis foul! He wanders about
in the storm, a filthy hovel his only place of shelter, until
he is deprived of that most precious gift of all—his reason.
There is, however, one consolation, he proves the preciousness of the despised love of Cordelia—that she at least was
faithful to her bond, though a little obstinate in her

expression of it. But Lear's happiness is not to last long; the villainous sisters deprive him of this his latest joy; their vile instrument, Edmund, gives the order for Cordelia's death, and the brightest and best of them all is mercilessly hung, while Lear dies with anguish of heart.

And these two monsters of ingratitude, what of them? It jars against our sense of justice that their wickedness should have the upper hand. Of the two, Goneril is the vilest, for she is the initiator of all the cruelty and crime. She has been truly described as a masculine woman, with a selfish visage and a dark frontlet. She seems to have no conscience, she has no misgivings; she spurns her husband for his milky gentleness; thinks him nothing but a moral fool, and treats her father's curses with a coolness terrible to think of. She is extremely selfish and jealous; when her father is got out of the way, she must have some other wicked thing to do, so she sets her mind on possessing the whole Kingdom, and her sister Regan must be got rid of. She betrothes herself to the villain Edmund while her husband is alive, poisons her own sister, plans the life of her husband, and finally destroys herself.

Regan is a much more feminine character; she is less fierce, and in her wickedness greatly dependant upon Goneril. She has some conscience, and trembles to draw her father's curses upon her. She, too, has fixed her affection on Edmund, but it is not before her husband's death, and this, perhaps, not so much because she loved him as to get advantage over her sister, for there was much rivalry, after all, between them. But Regan falls a victim to the viler hand of her unworthy sister.

EDMUND.

"With as much poisonous hypocrisie, desperate fraud, smooth malice, hidden ambition, and smiling envie, as in any living person could be harboured."

Sir Philip Sydney's ARCADIA.

Shakspere has interwoven with King Lear another story of ingratitude, the story of another father brought to ruin and misery by the ungrateful conduct of a son. But in this case Glo'ster suffers for a former sin of self-indulgence, while Lear was "far more sinned against than sinning." Glo'ster brings his misery upon himself, for he makes fun of the origin of his bastard son, keeps him away from home for nine years, and intends to send him out of the way again; in fact he has done everything that would tend to foster the spirit of hatred, deceit, and villainy in Edmund. His legitimate son Edgar has been far more reasonably treated, he has had all that home comfort could give him, but Edmund has been despised as an intruder in the family. There is no wonder then that he determines to be a villain, to be on an equal footing with his more favoured brother.

Edmund is Shakspere's typical villain, and perhaps his greatest hypocrite. He has all the boundless ambition of Richard III., and like him shrinks from no crime; he has the cynicism, treachery, and deceit of Iago to some extent developed in him. He has the same cause for discontent as Richard in the defect of his birth, though he is represented as having great outward beauty; he has much of Iago's "selfish calculation" and "cold reason" in the furtherance of his own ambitious designs; he has the same realistic free thinking and utter disbelief in all human virtue, the same indifference to the means which suit his purpose, the same hypocrisy which considers lack of dissimulation an unmanly thing and a weakness of the mind.

In his opening soliloquy he argues with himself upon the subject of his birth: wherefore is he "base" when he is as handsome, and as intelligent as his brother? And yet they brand him with that epithet base! But he will be equal with them, he will have his brother's land, and if his cunning invention only thrives "the base shall top the legitimate." He must first stir up ill-feeling between brother and father; and he writes a letter, feigning his brother's handwriting, to himself—purporting to be from his brother—suggesting conspiracy against the father, and hinting at the enjoyment they would have from his revenue. He sees his father coming towards him, and with well feigned innocence is reading the letter when Glo'ster enters. He pretends to be very reluctant to tell its contents, and when his father's indignation is stirred, he persuades him not to take action against his brother hastily, but to suspend his indignation until they have had better testimony of Edgar's intention, for after all, Edmund says, the brother may only be trying his affection towards their father. Edmund does this not so much to shield his brother, but finding his first plan serve him so well he would like more time to complete his evil schemes. Then he practises his deceit upon his brother, warns him against the father, and bids him go armed lest he be ill treated. Edgar unsuspectingly believes him, and keeps out of the way of his father, while Edmund takes advantage of Cornwall's unexpected arrival to make his brother fly from the place, gets up a sham fight, and when Edgar is gone wounds his own arm " to beget opinion of a fierce endeavour," and then tells his father that Edgar wounded him.

His brother out of the way Edmund must next be quit of his father; he is not satisfied to have gained possession of his brother's land, he must have his father's also. Glo'ster is touched at heart with the misfortunes of Lear, and he is determined to avenge his wrongs; he discloses his plans to Edmund, who, with fearful heartlessness, goes and betrays his father to Cornwall and Regan. This action, he says, will draw towards him :

> "That which my father loses, no less than all :
> The younger rises when the old doth fall."

Glo'ster's eyes are put out, and the villain inherits his lands and title. Surely he will be content now ? Not he ; success makes him bold, and he pushes on still further with his artful intrigues ; he covets now the land of Albany and Cornwall, the sons-in-law to Lear, and in order to gain them betrothes himself to both their wives. Cornwall is killed by mere accident, but Edmund and Goneril are baffled in their design for the murder of Albany, who stops their marriage.

Edmund has distinguished himself in the war against France, and has earned the loudest praises from the sisters, and even from Albany ; this over-elevates him, and forgetting his many evil deeds he challenges any one to prove him a traitor. Now Edgar, his wronged brother, he who, disguised, has been the faithful companion of his father in his wanderings, and has prevented his death, comes forward as the representative of truth and justice, to meet the villain with the sword. He, at any rate, in spite of Edmund's boasted strength—the eminence to which he has exalted

F

himself, his victor-sword and his ill earned fortune, he does not hesitate to tell Edmund:

> "Thou art a traitor,
> False to thy gods, thy brother, and thy father,
> Conspirant 'gainst this high illustrious prince,
> And from the extremest upward of thy head
> To the descent and dust below thy foot,
> A most toad-spotted traitor."

Edmund, however, is courageous enough to fight the avenger, but he falls a victim to the sword of the brother he has so cruelly wronged. Before he dies he confesses to have done all that Edgar charges him with, and more, much more, which time only will serve to show. Through the influence of Goneril he has ordered the death of Cordelia, to hang her in the prison; now he is wounded, he is anxious to withdraw his order, for there is blood enough on his head already. But it is too late; Cordelia is dead and in the arms of her heart-broken father.

University College of Wales,
    June, 1881.

THE SUPERNATURAL IN SHAKSPERE:
AND ITS USES.

"The poet's eye, in a fine frenzy rolling,
Doth glance from heaven to earth, from earth to heaven,
And, as imagination bodies forth
The forms of things unknown, the poet's pen
Turns them into shapes, and gives to airy nothing
A local habitation and a name.—*Midsummer Night's Dream.*

Act V. i. 13—17.

THE SUPERNATURAL IN SHAKSPERE.

There are many agencies at work which influence the
character of a man's life—agencies external and internal,
visible and invisible, manifest and mysterious. But amongst
them all the supernatural is perhaps the most powerful.
There is an inherent tendency in man to believe in that
which exceeds the terms of his own nature. His soul will
rise above itself in search of some higher, some ruling
power, to guide it through the vicissitudes of this life. The
most barbarous savage is conscious that there is something
in the universe which demands his recognition. He has no
real knowledge of it, nor of its attributes, but obeying
instinct he sets up some visible object, some likely symbol
of that higher power, and gives it his adoration. It is true
that civilization has produced men who have denied the
existence of any such Divine agency; men who have
believed in their own self-sufficiency to measure and to
comprehend all things; but the higher feelings of our nature
rebel against such assumption. The philosophy of the
Ancients supported this theory, but at the same time they
peopled the universe with celestial powers, who presided
over their actions and over the workings of nature. Jove
is seated on the summit of "cloud-capped Olympus," while
the minor gods charioteer in the sun, rule the tempests, and
rage in the storms. They wage war with each other; mix

with their chosen people in their conflicts; turn the
poisoned arrows of the enemy in their flight; and shield
their favourites from all harm.   Every department and
region of the world is full of their miraculous activity.
Above, they manage the thunders; below, they stir up
volcanic fires, and wrestle in the earthquakes.   The
universe itself is a vast arena in which these gods and
demi-gods are acting their parts.

In modern times a somewhat similar feeling has existed,
and to a certain extent exists still.   The idea that there is
some intermediate power between man and the Divine has
been very prevalent.   Men have been ready enough to
believe in fairies, ghosts, and witches, and even great and
cultured minds have been affected by such a belief.   Happily
reason and Christianity have done much to annihilate these
ancient superstitions; but after all we cannot but feel that
there is something still in nature which philosophy has to
fathom.

It is this intermediate phase of the supernatural which
is made use of by Shakspere.   The belief in witchcraft and
magic was very prevalent in his time.   This is, no doubt,
his main justification for employing it—a wish to gratify
the public taste.   There is, however, a worthier purpose
underlying, for it has been truly said that Shakepere never
wrote a line without a purpose.   His object was to illustrate
his story, to facilitate the working out of his plot, to bring
more forcibly to the minds of his hearers the truth of the
principles he wished to impart.   The manner in which he
accomplished his object remains for us to consider.   If we
were to grant that this phase of the supernatural really
existed, we should say that Shakspere had painted it most

naturally, for by the aid of his unbounded imagination and the wide range of his fancy he had the same insight into the supernatural that he had into the natural world. Our consideration of the subject will be confined to the most forcible examples as pictured in the plays *Midsummer Night's Dream*, *Macbeth*, *Hamlet*, and *The Tempest*.

The first of these is, as its name implies, simply a dream —full of marvel, surprise, splendour, and flourish. The poet's great characteristic is here laid aside; instead of natural impulse, flowing from real life and characters, caprice—the pursuit of fairies and elves—reigns supreme. He does not seem to endow these blithe spirits with any powers of mind, for nowhere is reflection imparted to them. They are the embodiment of fancy, freak, and frolic. They interfere at every turn with the real characters of the play: careless and unscrupulous they lead men and women into error and place them in opposite relations. They live a most luxurious and merry life—

> Over hill, over dale,
> Through bush, through briar,

they scamper. They sing, and they dance, while their ringlets float in the whistling wind. They sleep in the beauteous dells of flowers, lulled by the sweet scent of the musk rose, and the luxurious woodbine; and when they wake

> Pluck the wings from painted butterflies,
> To fan the moonbeams from their sleeping eyes.

They seek the friendship of the nightingale and all the lovelier birds, but wage a sprightly war with the uglier creatures of bats, owls, and hedgehogs. Led by Puck, the prince of mischief in Fairyland, they pursue their wanton

tricks, and make fearful havoc with the lovers, whom they
perplex with opposite interests, and then "esteem it sport
to see them jangle." They torment decrepid old age, and
sipping gossips; skim the house-wife's milk, and take
delight in punishing sluts and sluttery. Night-mares and
dreams are under their control; they mislead the night
wanderer, and then laugh at his confusion when he awakes.
But their tricks are not confined to men, they play their
pranks upon each other. By virtue of the juice of a
favourite flower, the jealous Oberon compels the fair Titinia
to dote upon the quaint old Bottom, adorned by Puck with
"an ass's nowl,"—to think him wise and beautiful, to give
him fairy attendance and fairy courtesy.* In the end,
however, all things are transformed, all mistakes rectified,
all hopes consummated in the happiest manner, and Puck
entreats us to think it all a dream.

But what is the purpose which underlies it all? Of
what use to us is this dream? The poet's object was to
portray certain capricious characters which, unfortunately,
exist in the world,—to bring before his hearers the mischievous influence of such beings, and their relation with
other mortals. Such types of humanity are not difficult to
find, even in the society of our own day—men and women
altogether insensible of the higher interests of life, devoid of
serious thought, reckless and careless in all their actions.
They can admire the beautiful, the agreeable, and the
fantastic, but they shrink from grappling with the earnest,
the real, and the difficult. Their whole life is one of
pleasure and romance; they delight in deceiving; they are

---

* Compare Essay on Shakspere's Clowns—Second period—The
Mechanics.

very skilful in acting artificial parts, in assuming appearances, and in making life one string of festivity, sport, and
jest. These sylphlike creatures have no higher aim than to
torment and irritate mankind; and these Shakspere has
chosen with remarkable skill as the originals "from whose
fixed characteristics he has given form and life to his airy
spirits."

There is a strange difference between *Midsummer Night's
Dream* and the tragedy of *Macbeth*, and there is a strange
contrast, too, in the supernatural agents employed in them.
Instead of caprice and fantasy, base and cruel ingratitude
—"ingratitude more strong than traitors' arms"—is the
theme for the poet's power. Macbeth receives a venerable
monarch, and a near kinsman, under his roof, with well
feigned hospitality, and then murders him with his own
hands in order to usurp his throne. The subject, indeed, is
a black one, and in less skilful hands would have little
attractiveness; but *Macbeth* has been called by Drake "the
most sublime and impressive drama the world has ever
beheld: the greatest effort of our author's genius." We are
transported into the Highlands of Scotland, where everything seems tinged with superstition: "with tangible inter-
communication with the supernatural world." Instead of
the merry revels of the fairies, we have the hideous work of
the witches; harmless tricks are replaced by cruel and
wicked temptations. Merited praise has often been
bestowed upon the powerful representation of these weird
spirits, and their incantations. They are unquestionably
among the most wonderful of the imaginative inventions
of our poet. Their first appearance on the scene gives the
key-note to the whole drama—

Fair is foul, and foul is fair,
Hover through the fog, and filthy air.

They meet in thunder, lightening, hail, and rain, upon the blasted heath to plan their wicked schemes. Withered, wild, and weather-beaten in appearance, sexless, and ugly as the evil-one, "they look not like the inhabitants of the earth and yet are on it." They are utterly devoid of human sympathy, their whole delight is in evil,—to tempt a wayward and ambitious son. They make him spurn fate, and scorn death; they spur him on in his wicked course against all reason, and without fear. These terrible creatures "tangle in every fibre with evil energy; they are souls of sin springing up into everlasting death; they have their raptures, and their ecstacies in crime." What could be more hideous than the scene in the dark cave, where, in the boiling cauldron they make their foul "hell-broth" with all that is vile, unclean, and venomous. They ape the harmless dance of the fairies as they caper around, enchanting the foul ingredients as they throw them in. These secret, black, and midnight hags can find no name vile enough for their deeds. When Macbeth asks them to foretell his fate, they encourage him to be bloody, bold, and resolute: to laugh to scorn the power of man; they warn him against his enemy Macduff, whom alone he has to fear; but in the eagerness of the moment he pays little heed to their warning, and spurred on by their encouraging prophecies he dashes on to his deeds of blood.

It is comparatively difficult to arrive at any definite conclusions respecting Shakspere's purpose in his impersonation of the witches, and many theories have been put forth on the subject. Gervinus says of them "they are not the avengers in a deed, but the tempters to it, the panderers of sin." Lamb believes that they generated deeds of blood, and originated the evil impulses of the soul; and Schlegel maintains that Macbeth sunk under a deep-laid hellish temptation, and under their supernatural impulses. It cannot, however, be said that the witches represent the whole nature of Macbeth, nor that they have an independent existence. It is most probable that Shakspere intended them to represent that peculiar kind of temptation to which man is subjected,—temptation which at one time seems to originate in ourselves, and at another to be suggested by some external influence. In so far as man yields to this temptation he makes it his own, but at the same time its first suggestion may come from some power outside himself. This seems to be the peculiar position of Macbeth, and Shakspere has given us in a plastic form this mystery in nature which is so difficult to solve,—where do these evil suggestions come from? Recognizing the difficulty of this question our conception of the character of Macbeth must be very carefully estimated. If all the promptings to crime of which he is guilty originated in himself his character would indeed be a black one. He would seem to be the victim of developed passion with full mastery over him; but if we remember that there are external influences at work spurring him on in his evil deeds, this estimate of him will require considerable modification. He does not come before us as completely under the influence of unbridled passion and inordinate ambition. We have in Macbeth a man capable of accomplishing much good as well as much evil. He has no need to encourage in himself the inspiring promises of the witches; ample room is left for the exercise of his own will. This is evident from the fact that Banquo saw the witches too, and was equally tempted by them, but his firmer will enabled him to withstand their temptings. Macbeth listens to them, and the goodness of his nature is gradually overcome by the evil. He is very undecided in his action at first, and his wife, Lady Macbeth, says that his nature is

> Too full of the milk of human kindness
> To catch the nearest way.

Lady Macbeth is fully decided in her action. She is fully bent upon the crime. She bids Macbeth to screw up his courage to the sticking place, and urges him on to the bloody deed. His complex nature compels him to decide for the good or for the evil, and ultimately the evil is triumphant. This gives him his great decision, and he goes on boldly and assuredly to the murderous work.

Shakspere in this play uses the supernatural agencies to picture more strikingly the sad effects of pandering with, or giving way to evil temptations. In the end Macbeth meets the great avenger, Macduff, the only one he had to fear, and then the cowardliness of his evil nature manifests itself. " My soul is too much charged with blood of thine already" escapes from him as he shrinks under the piercing and revengeful look of Macduff. His hitherto undaunted courage forsakes him, and he falls a victim to his evil passion. Thus Shakspere shows very forcibly how justice must sooner or later visit with its sternest hand those who revel in deeds of blood.

Hamlet is an agreeable change after considering so cruel a plot as *Macbeth.* In Hamlet, the Prince of Denmark, we have the predominance of the contemplative over the practical in a mind of the highest order, both intellectually and morally. He is placed in the most trying circumstances. He is heir apparent to the throne; his father has died very suspiciously, and his mother thrusts him—her only son—from the crown by marrying his dead father's brother.* It is a questioned point as to whether Hamlet knew or suspected that his father had been murdered by his uncle. If he did, he takes no steps to punish the murderer. He is too abstracted; but when his mother marries his uncle, "but two months" after his father's death, he seems to realize his position. In the solitude of his thought he pours forth, with all the agony of his soul, that most impassioned address:—

> Oh, that this too, too solid flesh would melt,
> Thaw, and resolve itself into a dew.

He loses himself again in meditation—how weary, stale, flat, and unprofitable seem to him all the uses of the world—and again he delays to take action. Shakspere, therefore, has recourse to supernatural power in order to rouse Hamlet to a sense of the injustice he is suffering. But he does this not by the playful trick of the fairy, nor yet by the inspiring prophecy of the witch. The mind of Hamlet is too sensitive, too critical for either; he must have something more convincing, "an honest ghost," the spirit of his father. The poet prepares Hamlet for receiving the sad and strange story by preliminary appearances of the ghost to Horatio. After relating his sufferings in an imaginary purgatory, the spirit unfolds the sad tale of his murder—a murder "most foul, strange, and unnatural"—

---

*Compare Shakspere's Hypocrites—the King in *Hamlet*.

how he was cut off from the world by his own brother, even in the blossoms of his sin, with no reckoning made, but sent to his account with all his imperfections on his head. He speaks of the deceitfulness of his wife, but leaving her to Heaven and to "those fires that in her bosom lodge to prick and sting her," he pleads with his son, in the name of the love that he has for an affectionate father, to avenge him. Hamlet, on the impulse of the moment, is eager to learn more, so that with "wings swift as meditation" he may sweep to his revenge. The father reveals all; but does the son carry out his resolve? No! He must needs meditate again; he must reason with himself as to the justice of taking revenge:—

> Whether 'tis nobler in the mind
> To suffer the slings and arrows of outrageous fortune,
> Or to take up arms against a sea of troubles,
> And by opposing end them.

How can he justify such a deed to the world? How can he vindicate in himself a crime which he must lodge against another? He has no spirit of revenge about him, he cannot satisfy himself that there is any justice in it. He delays taking action; puts it off until some more convenient time. He meditates again, and reproaches himself for his inertness, but still he takes no steps to gratify his father's wish. We cannot, however, charge Hamlet with cowardice or want of courage. All his inaction must be attributed to the critical, the contemplative nature of his mind, and his utter aversion to the spirit of revenge.

The great lesson to be learned from the use of the supernatural in *Hamlet* is, *the importance of action;* that this is the chief end of our existence; that all our faculties, all our intellectual powers are rather misfortunes to us than otherwise, if they keep us from duty. In Hamlet we have a character in whom all that is amiable and excellent is combined, but he lives in meditation, his whole life is dwindled away by "continually resolving to do, yet doing nothing but resolve." And this failing of Hamlet may be placed to the general account of humanity. All his distress, his abstractedness, his depression, his laxity in action, may be applied to ourselves, as well as the unhappy results which spring therefrom.

The Tempest has been placed in the final period of Shakspere's writings, and very justly so. The manner in which it is worked out, especially that part which we have to consider, shows that Shakspere was no longer in his apprenticeship, but that he had reached the zenith of his power. In his latter days the poet seems to have been much engaged with the ingratitude of men: how we are to receive the injuries inflicted on us by others.* The story of *The Tempest* is one of rebellion and usurpation by one brother against another,—an ungrateful brother against a beneficent one. And in Prospero Shakspere has pictured the noblest attitude a brother so wronged could take: an attitude of forbearance and forgiveness. To impart these lessons more forcibly, the poet has recourse to the supernatural. Still adhering to popular belief, he takes advantage of the strange stories related by travellers of the wonders in newly discovered quarters of the globe. In the character of Prospero he portrays a venerable Magician, who has complete power over the spirit world on a desert

---

* Compare Shakspere's Clowns—conclusion of Third Period.

island in the Bermudas. But the supernatural agents in this work are of quite a superior order. It is no longer as in Shakspere's youth when men and women were mere toys for fairy pranks, nor as in Macbeth, where man submits to the evil promptings of the witches; the poet has a higher purpose in view. In Ariel we have a spirit whose mission it is to help and encourage man in the nobler deeds of mercy and forgiveness. And to accomplish his work Prospero has under his command spirits which rule the four elements. By their aid he bedims the noonday sun, calls forth the mutinous winds, lashes the sea into furious war, gives fire to the rattling thunder, and bids the earth yield forth her dead. In Ariel, however, Shakspere embodies the power of all these minor spirits. First, he appears as a sea nymph, swimming and careering on the foamy waves; then as a spirit of fire, diving into flame; and then as a spirit of earth, penetrating its heated veins. But his real nature is (as his name implies) that of a Sylph, a spirit of the air. In this shape he is pictured as riding on the curled clouds; running on the sharp winds, while he pursues his mission to deceive, to scatter, and to frighten evil-doers. He has much more freedom than the rest of the spirits. Prospero bids him do his will, but leaves the spirit to choose the method; and in every case he serves his master faithfully and well—without a mistake, grudge or grumble.

It is not difficult to find Shakspere's object in using the supernatural here; it is plainly as Dowden puts it,—"The winning back to good of souls given to evil." The spirit Ariel represents Prospero's self—his truest nature. His throne usurped by a brother, and banished to a desert island, his finer character developes itself. His brother, at last, comes within his power, he can deprive him of his life, of all, if he wishes, but does he let vindictiveness possess him? No. He sends the spirit Ariel—his own nobler will—on a mission of forgiveness, to bring his brother to repentance. In the wide extent of Ariel's exploits through the spirit world we have the extensive field of usefulness in which a character such as Prospero's can employ itself. In Ariel's pleading for freedom we recognize Prospero's wish to be relieved from the anxieties of this life; he feels that, like the spirits over which he has such complete control, he too must vanish into "thin and empty air;" that

> "We are all such stuff
> As dreams are made of, and our little life
> Is rounded by a sleep."

Considering the supernatural in Shakspere as a whole we have seen that his main justification for its use is that the age in which he lived believed very much in it; but at the same time he had something more in view than simply the gratification or the amusement of his audience. He employed it as a symbol of the most natural relations, and thus appealed to his hearers much more powerfully. We have seen how in *Midsummer Night's Dream* the fairies represent those capricious, whimsical, fantastical characters whose only aim is their own enjoyment, and who seek to accomplish this end by mortifying and tormenting humanity; how in *Macbeth* the witches mirror those viler temptations which spur men on to cursed and wicked deeds; how in *Hamlet* the spirit of a murdered father pleads with the sluggish soul of a too meditative son, seeking to rouse him

---

* Compare Carlyle—"But whence?—O! Heaven, whither? Sense knows not; Faith knows not; only that it is through Mystery to Mystery, from God to God."—SARTOR RESARTUS, *Book iii., cp. 9.*

G

to action in the cause of justice; how in the *Tempest* Ariel, representing Prospero's better nature, seeks to bring remorse to an erring and ungrateful brother, and in the end to give him pardon. In the *Dream* the supernatural agents have man completely under their control; in *Hamlet* and *Macbeth* they are co-agents with man, and in the *Tempest* they are altogether under man's control. And all this is worked out with so much skill, such form, character, and consistency is given to this ideal supernatural world that "nature seems elevated above herself," the impossible is brought into the region of the possible, and through it all our reason is never offended. We cannot but admire the underlying purpose of our author; and we cannot but believe that he fulfilled his purpose in a manner impossible to any but himself.

SHAKSPERE'S CLOWNS.

Now Mercury endue thee with leasing, for thou speakest well of fools.

Twelfth Night. Act 1. v. 95.

O! that I were a fool!
I am ambitious for a motley coat,
To speak my mind ; and I will through and through
Cleanse the foul body of the infected world,
If they will patiently receive my medicine.

Jacques (*As you like it*). Act II. vii. 42—60.

Wit, an't be thy will, put me into good fooling! Those wits that think they have thee, do very oft prove fools; and I, that am sure I lack thee, may pass for a wise man: for what says Quinapalus? Better a witty fool, than a foolish wit.

Twelfth Night. Act I. v. 30—34.

SHAKSPERE'S CLOWNS.

Shakspere was the most universal genius that ever lived —a fact often asserted, and seldom, if ever, contradicted. The more we read of him the more its truth is impressed upon us. There seems to be no phase of human existence upon which he has not placed his finger. He has the same "absolute command over our laughter and our tears, all the resources of passion, wit, of thought, of observation; he has the same unbounded range of fanciful invention, whether terrible or playful; the same insight into the world of imagination as he has into the world of reality." * And not only this: he is the most original genius that ever lived. The poetry of Shakspere was inspiration: indeed he is not so much an imitator as an instrument of nature; and it is not so just to say that he speaks *from* her, as that she speaks *through* him. His characters are so much nature herself, that it is a sort of injury to call them by so distant a name as copies of her †.

And one of the most original branches of Shakspere's art is the comic element, in which he has indulged so freely, and with such power. For Shakspere could laugh, he could laugh heartily; and this, we have been told, is a comforting fact to be borne in mind, a fact which serves to

---

* Hazlitt—"Shakspere's Characters."   † Pope.

rescue us from the domination of intense and narrow
natures, who claim authority by virtue of their grasp of one
half the realities of our existence, and their denial of the
rest.   The wit and humour of Shakspere, like his total
genius, is many-sided : he knew every nook and corner
of it, every quip and quirk, every quiditty and oddity
capable of moving any laughter-loving man.   His power
of wit and repartee is forcibly told by Fuller:—"Many
were the *wit-combates* betwixt him and *Ben Johnson*;
which two I behold like a *Spanish great Galleon*,
and an *English man of War*: Master *Johnson* (like the
former) was built far higher in Learning; *solid* but *slow*
in his performances.   *Shakespear*, with the *English Man of
War*, lesser in *bulk*, but lighter in *sailing*, could turn with
all tides, tack about, and take advantage of all winds by the
quickness of his Wit and Invention.*   Shakspere abounds
in kindly mirth—"he can dandle a fool as tenderly as any
nurse qualified to take a baby from the birth, can deal with
her charge."   Through his clowns and fools the poet scoffs
at the world, and yet remains aloof from its interests; he
smiles at human greatness, and yet pays homage to the
great; he makes fun of human love and human joy, and yet
they are deeply real to him; he jokes with human sorrow,
but he enters into the deepest anguish of the soul; he sees
through it all, and knows that it has an end and a quietus.
This comic genius of Shakspere has been compared to the
bee, in its power to extract honey from weeds and poisons,
rather than in its power of leaving a sting behind it.   He
gives a most amusing exaggeration to the prevailing foibles

* Fuller: "The History of the Worthies of England"—Quoted
in "Shakspere's Centurie of Prayse."—N. S. S. papers, 1879.

of his characters, and in such a way that they themselves, instead of being offended at it, are inclined to join in the fun; he contrives opportunities for such characters to shew themselves off in the happiest light, rather than render them contemptible in the perverse construction of the wit or malice of others. Thus we understand how it is that he allows folly to shoot out and grow with such unchecked luxuriance. He gives absurdity every encouragement, and nonsense room to flourish in. He runs riot in conceits, and idolizes a quibble: his whole object is to turn the meanest and rudest objects to pleasurable account. The relish which he has of a pun, or the quaint humour of a low character, does not interfere with the delight with which he describes a beautiful image, or the most refined sentiment. Touchstone and Jacques in no way disturb the picture of the beautiful Rosalind: we have additional pleasure from her quick wit and good sense through their railings; the clowns do not spoil the sweetness of the character of Viola, nor the purity and faithfulness of Desdemona.

But we must say something of these Clowns as they existed in real life. Fools and Jesters have had their place in all times and in all countries: they reached the culminating point of their influence in the middle ages, when they had a recognized place and recognized functions in the social organism. They were not only naturally inclined and endowed with qualities for the amusement of others, but they used their powers, or weaknesses, as a regular means of getting a livelihood. Savage Jugglers, Medicinemen, and Pardoners have much in common with the Fools and Jesters by profession. There existed in ancient Greece a distinct class of professional Fools, whose

habits very much resembled those of the Jesters of the
middle ages.*   It was the same in Rome, and Fools have
existed from time immemorial at the Eastern courts.   On
the conquest of Mexico, Court Fools and deformed creatures
of all kinds were found at the court of Montezuma, who
believed that more instruction could be gathered from them
than from court favourites, for they dared to tell the truth.
The dress of the regular Court Fool was not altogether a
rigid uniform—it seems to have changed considerably from
time to time.   The head was shaved, the coat motley, the
breeches tight and generally one leg different in colour
from the other.   The head was covered with a piece
resembling a monk's cowl, which fell over the breast and
shoulders, and often bore asses ears, and was crested with a
coxcomb, while small bells hung from various parts of the
attire.   The fool's bauble was a short staff, bearing a
ridiculous head, to which was sometimes attached an
inflated bladder, by means of which sham castigations were
inflicted.   A long petticoat was also occasionally worn, but
this seems to have belonged rather to the idiots than to the
wits, for some of these fools were chosen to excite laughter
from their deformity of mind or body, while others were
chosen for a certain alertness, and power of repartee—these
were the buts and wits.   The Fool's business was to amuse
his master, to excite him to laughter by witty comparison
and sharp contrast, to prevent the over-oppression of state
affairs, and, in harmony with the well-known physiological
precept, by his liveliness at meals, to assist his lord's
digestion.   In England the list of Court Fools is a long

* Xenophon gives a picturesque account of one of these in
The Banquet.

one—from Hitard, the Fool of Edmund Ironside, to Muckle
John, the Fool of Charles I., probably the last official Royal
Fool. The private Fool existed as late as last century, as is
proved by Swift's epitaph on Dicky Pearce, the Earl of
Suffolk's Jester. The type still exists in its lowest and
most burlesque form as the Fool of the travelling circus and
the comic Clown of the pantomime.

Shakspere invariably held up the mirror to the age in
which he lived: every prevailing habit and usage of his
time was seized for the purpose of his art; and the Fool
received his special attention. The function of the Clown
on the stage had been much abused—more license had been
taken with this than any other character. The Fool's part
was generally written out, but he was allowed to alter it as
he wished, to introduce extempore jokes, and the scenes
were often stretched out until the comic elements of the
play predominated.* Shakspere at once set his mark upon
the practice, and he determined to dignify the character
and rescue it from its deplorable condition. But from the
coarseness of the actors and the fostered inclination of the
people to laugh solely at the clumsy, ludicrous jokes of the
Clown, his task was a difficult one. Gervinus mentions
what a misuse of the privileges of the Clown Tarlton and
Kempe made upon the stage; and as long as this continued,
as long as the principal art of these actors, and the principal
pleasure of the public was that they should stretch out the
chin, let their arms hang lose, and twirl their wooden
swords, Shakspere could hardly venture to bring a more
refined character of this sort upon the stage. Kempe twice

---

* Compare Marlowe's *Dr. Faustus*.

withdrew from the company at the Blackfriars Theatre, and
it was only when he and his like were removed that
Shakspere could write that more refined programme in
Hamlet for the actor of the Fool. Although our poet
indulged his comic vein quite as liberally as any other, he
reprobates at once both the dramatist and the actor for
thus degrading his art and his subject by inopportune
drollery. He admits the important and leading function of
the Clown, but he restricts the actor to the part written
down for him. At the same time he gives a rule of
restriction to the dramatist also:

> "And let those that play your clowns speak no more than is set down for them,
> for there be of them that will themselves laugh, to set on some quantity of barren
> spectators to laugh too; though in the mean time some necessary question of the
> play be then to be considered: that is villainous, and shews a most pitiful ambition
> in the fool that uses it."
>
> *Hamlet —to the Players. Act III. ii. 39—46.*

Shakspere ascribes the highest value to these Fools and
men of wit, and he gives them full and unlimited power to
speak the truth, to rend asunder as often as they will the
veil of mere propriety and hypocrisy, and wittily to unmask
the folly of others under the cover of their own folly. This
appeared to the poet "a practice as full of labour as a wise
man's art," and as useful as a preacher's discourse. To use
properly and wisely the sting of seeming folly belonged to
the most expert knowledge of the world and of men—"of the
quality of persons and the time," for men in general he
considered the presence of the Fool as a very useful test of
head and heart. And so far as Shakspere's art is concerned
he rendered complete homage to the notion of the age that
the Fool had something of a divine and foretelling nature in
him: hence his elevation of the character. He often invests
his simple Clown with a deeper significance than his main

characters in the piece, giving him power to solve almost unconsciously problems of life over which the wise have laboured without profit.

In the treatment of the subject we shall distinguish three periods in the growth of Shakspere's art as shewn in his Fools :—

First—The Tentative or Experimental period, chiefly noticeable for its verbal jokes, with its representative clown Launce.

Second—The Ambidexterous or Vivacious period, with its mirth and laughter-loving innocence, as opposed to sentimentalism, and its representative Touchstone.

Third—The Soul-stirring and Censorious, with its finest and fullest development of Shakspere's clowns in *King Lear*— almost the last faithful creature of the ruined king.

FIRST PERIOD.

TENTATIVE—YOUNGMANISH—LOQUACIOUS.

I.—CHARACTERISTICS.

II.—LAUNCE AND SPEED.
(Two Gentlemen of Verona.)

III.—LOVE'S LABOUR LOST.
(Costard.)

IV.—LAUNCELOT GOBBO.
(Merchant of Venice.)

V.—THE MECHANICS.
(Midsummer Night's Dream.)

FIRST PERIOD.

The clowns and fools of this period present the same characteristics as the rest of Shakspere's early work—they are merely sketched. This is the period of experiments ; as yet he is deficient in the subjects of deep thought and emotion, he has not got a thorough grasp of life. Still all his work is marked by his extraordinary mental gifts, his vivacity, his cleverness, and his delight in the beautiful. He took pleasure in the mere play of his wits ; he had felt none of the graver influences of life. With his high spirits he could enjoy fun pure and simple ; he was full of comic surprises and grotesque incidents ; his satire consists solely in gay attacks upon the superficial oddities, follies, and affectations of the world. He shews us through his first-period Fools the pleasure which he derived from the quick encounter of his wits, from the bandying of a jest to and fro in the air, until at last it falls into an elaborate play of words—"Now, by the salt we have of the Mediterranean, a sweet touch : a quick venew of wit : snip, snap. quick, and home : it rejoiceth my intellect." The comic and the serious. the tender and the sentimental elements of the drama exist side by side, and serve as a kind of criticism each upon the other : the lover convicts the clown of insensibility to the higher facts of life ; the clown convicts the lover of blind-

ness or extravagance of passion. The elements do not as yet
interpenetrate; one set of personages is reserved for the
grave or tender business of the drama, and a different set of
personages is told off to the comic business. Afterwards we
shall see how they intermingle.

SPEED AND LAUNCE *(Two Gentlemen of Verona).*

Here the comic part of the business is entrusted to a pair
of clowns, servants of Valentine and Proteus, to whom they
are placed in characteristic opposition—the witty Speed to
the amiable Valentine, awkward Launce to clever Proteus—
and, by actions of their own, exist as a kind of parody by
the side of the main characters of the piece. Launce's
account of his farewell is a parody on Juliet's silent parting
with Proteus. The scene in which Speed "thrust himself"
into Launce's love affairs caricatures the false intrusion of
Proteus into Valentine's love. And the scenes of Launce
and his dog Crab, which will occur to the general reader as
most offensive, have been shown to have a still deeper
meaning. To this silly, semi-brute man, who sympathizes
with his beast more than with men, his dog is his best friend.
He has received stripes for this dog, taken his faults upon
him; he has been willing to sacrifice everything for him;
and at last even this friend he will resign, his best possession
he will abandon to do service to his master. With this
capacity for sacrifice, this simple child of nature is placed
by the side of that splendid model of manly endowments,
Proteus, who, self-seeking, betrayed friend and lover. And
then this fine relation of the lower to the higher parts of the

piece is so skillfully concealed by the removal of all moralizing from the action, that the cultivated examiner of the play finds the objective effect of the action in no wise interfered with, while the groundling of the pit tastes unimpeded his pure delight in common nature.*

Both the clowns are shrewder than their masters. Speed, who is the professed wit, and skilled at " word-matching " and making puns, recognizes the love of Silvia before Valentine ; he knows his master to be in love almost before he knows it himself, for he says—

" You have learned, like Sir Proteus, to wreath your arms, like a malcontent ; to relish a love-song, like a robin redbreast ; to walk alone, like one that had the pestilence ; to sigh, like a schoolboy that had lost his A B C ; to weep, like a young wench that had buried her grandam ; to fast, like one that takes diet ; to watch, like one that fears robbing ; to speak, puling like a beggar at Hallowmas. You were wont, when you laughed, to crow like a cock ; when you walked, to walk like one of the lions ; when you fasted, it was presently after dinner ; when you looked sadly, it was for want of money ; and now you are metamorphosed with a mistress, that, when I look on you, I can hardly think you my master."

Act II. i. 17—30.

They discuss together the virtues of Silvia ; Valentine says that her beauty is exquisite and her favour infinite, which, Speed retorts, is " because the one is painted, and the other out of count "—she is so painted to make her fair that no man counts of her beauty. But it does not matter at all what she looks like, for " Love is blind," and Valentine can see no defects.

Launce is the broad humorist who blunders into matter of a more vital, more pregnant kind than the tongue of Speed can command. With his dog Crab, a most important personage in this play, and his not less important stick, Launce leads the procession of Shakspere's Clowns, and there march behind him in a straggling train as well nigh

---

* Gervinus.— *Vide* Shakespeare Commentaries.

H

motley a crew of mirth-provoking, side-splitting Fools as one
could think of. The scenes of Launce and his dog are
inimitable in the way of farcical drollery and invention.
Just think of this dog's ungratefulness in the parting
scene ! Here has Launce been weeping for an hour, his
mother weeping too, his father wailing, his sister crying, the
maid howling, the cat wringing her hands, and all the house
in great perplexity, yet, this cruel-hearted cur all the while
shed not a tear, nor spoke a word : surely he was the sour-
est-natured dog alive ; he is a stone, a very pebble-stone,
and hath no pity in him ; why a Jew would have wept to
have seen such a parting, but this dog shed not a tear.
The mischievous little pup is equally troublesome when
sent as a present to Mistress Silvia, and it is very provoking
after the bringing-up he has had. " Oh ! it is a foul thing
when a cur cannot keep himself in all companies !"   For
Launce had taught him even as one would say expressly
·"thus I would teach my dog;" he had saved him from
drowning, sat in the stocks for the puddings he had stolen,
stood in the pillory for the geese he had killed, and yet
withal this little beast could not behave himself.

The scene where Speed "thrusts himself into the secrets"
of Launce is equally amusing, for Launce is very deeply in
love, so deep that a team of horses could not pluck him
from it, and in love too with a woman, a maiden.   And
she has many Christian qualities in addition to her domestic
virtues : she talks in her sleep, which is much better than
sleeping in her talk; she is slow in words—surely woman's
only virtue; she has no teeth, but no matter *(n'importe)*
he likes crusts; she has more hair than wit, more faults
than hairs, and more wealth than faults—and that latter

word makes all her faults gracious, so he will have her, come what may. Launce gets Speed into trouble for interesting himself so much in this love-affair, and rejoices in it; he looks forward with pleasure to a sight of the boy's correction, and he will stand aside to enjoy the completion of the fun.

LOVE'S LABOUR LOST *(Costard)*.

This play is entirely Shakspere's invention, and, says Hazlitt, if we were to part with any of his comedies, it would be this. Still we should be loth to part with Don Andrean de Armado, that mighty potentate of nonsense, or his page, that handful of wit; with Nathaniel, the curate, or Holofernes, the schoolmaster, with Costard, the clown, or Dull, the constable. So he thinks we had better let the play stand as it is, and not venture " to set a mark of reprobation upon it." So far as we are concerned, it matters little, for Costard has no attraction : he does nothing but turn a phrase now and then, and pollute it with his "odd taint of endemic contagion." The whole comedy concerns itself with " self-culture," and the poet takes the opportunity of having his laugh at the fashionable affectations of the time.

LAUNCELOT GOBBO *(Merchant of Venice)*.

Launcelot bears the same relation to the main characters of the piece as we have noticed with Launce and Speed. The scene between Launcelot and his father is a parody upon the scene between Jessica and her's. Launcelot's dialogue with his conscience and the fiend is very amusing, and it proves him after all to be an honest fellow. The fiend tempts him to run away from the Jew, while his conscience bids him stay, and ultimately he yields to the fiend, who, he says, gives him better counsel, for though he could live better in the house of the rich old Jew, yet his sense of honour bids him go and live with the poor generous man. On the way he plays a prank with his father, but we feel that after all it is not from an unkind heart.

THE MECHANICS (*Midsummer Night's Dream*).

We recognize at once, in the "rude mechanicals," an advance in Shakspere's comic art. Hitherto all the poet's faculties have been accustomed to go to work separately : now they are beginning to approach one another. Here, Bottom, the weaver, and Titinia, the fairy, meet—the humour enriches itself by coalescing with the fancy; the comic is no longer purely comic, "it is a mingled web, shot through by the beautiful." At a subsequent period, when the highest powers of the poet are aroused, we shall see how all his faculties have become fused together.

Bottom is unquestionably a finer comic than any preceding character we have noticed. How lean and impoverished his fellows, the Athenian craftsmen, find themselves in the presence of this many-sided genius, Nick Bottom ! Rarely is a great artist appreciated in the degree that he is—" he hath simply the best head of any handicraftman in Athens ; yea, and the best person too; he is a very paramour for a sweet voice." With what a

magnificent multiplicity of gifts he is endowed! How vast
has the bounty of nature been to him! And he has a fine
set of companions—

> " A crew of patches, rude mechanicals,
> That work for bread upon Athenian stalls."
>
> *Act III. Sc. I.*

There is Quince, the carpenter; Snug, the joiner; Flute, the
bellows-mender; Snout, the tinker; and Starvelling, the
tailor. But Bottom is very conceited and fantastical, and
in calling over the rôle for the coming play, he is ready to
undertake anything, as if it was as much a matter of course
as the motion of his loom and shuttle. First of all Quince
assigns to him the part of Pyramus—"a lover that kills
himself most gallantly for love. Then let the audience
look to their eyes, for Bottom can move storms—he can
condole in some measure. Still he prefers to play the
tyrant, "the Ercles' vein, is more to his humour. Flute
does not like to play a woman's part because he has a beard
coming, but, no matter, Bottom will undertake it, "an I may
hide my face, let me play Thisby too. I will speak in a
monstrous little voice—' Thisne, Thisne, --Ah! Pyramus,
my lover dear! thy Thisby dear, and lady dear! " And
as for the lion's part, alloted to the bashful Snug, why he
will take that too—" I will roar, that I will do any man's
heart good to hear me : I will roar that I will make the
Duke say, let him roar again, let him roar again." This
being objected to as improper, for he would frighten the
Duchess and the ladies, he has still a resource in the good
opinion of himself—" I will roar as gently as any sucking
dove : I will roar you an't were any nightingale." But
from all these wild dreams of universal ambition he is

recalled by the less presumptious Quince to his proper
impersonation, "You can play no part but Pyramus."
And this wonderful genius who rules the roast amongst his
fellow mechanics is quite as much at home in his new
character of the ass of Titinia--with his amiable cheeks and
fair large ears.* All at once he acquires a most learned
taste, and grows fastidious in everything. He thinks he
will to the barber's, for he is such a tender ass that if his
hair do but tickle him he must needs scratch ; he has a good
reasonable ear for music :—"let us have the tongues and
bones ; " and as for eating he has a great desire for a bottle
of hay—good, sweet hay,—and a handful or two of sweet
peas. He is quite as familiar with his new fairy attendants,
and assigns them their part with due gravity:—"Monsieur
Cobweb, get your weapons in your hand, and kill me a red-
hipped humble-bee, on the top of a thistle, and good
monsieur bring me a honey-bag." But when he awakes he
is rather surprised ; what a rare vision he has had !—past
the wit of man to say what dream it was : a man was but
an ass if he go about and try to expound it. "The eye of
man hath not heard, the ear of man hath not seen, man's
hand is not able to taste, his tongue to conceive, nor his
heart to report, what my dream was. I will get to Peter
Quince to write a ballad of this dream : it shall be called
Bottom's dream, because it hath no bottom." Then when
they come to play before the duke, Bottom proves himself
to be as much a stage-manager as he is an actor. He
conceives the device for obviating the danger of frightening
the ladies by writing a prologue to describe the killing of

* Compare the essay on "The Supernatural in Shakspere."

Pyramus ; moonshine is to be represented by opening a window or else one must come in with a bush of thorns and a lanthorn : and Snout must stand to represent a wall, and open his fingers for a cranny hole through which the lover's must whisper.

This play acted by the clowns is the reverse of the poet's own work, which demands all the spectator's reflective and imitative fancy to open to him this aerial world ; whilst in the other nothing at all is left to the imagination of the spectator. This great contrast between the rough mechanics and the tender and delicate fairies, between the awkward and the beautiful, the real and the truly imaginative, gives greater prominence to both.

SECOND PERIOD.

AMBIDEXTEROUS—MIRTH-LAUGHTER-LOVING—VIVACIOUS.

I.—CHARACTERISTICS.

II.—CLOWN.

(All's well that end's well.)

III.—FESTE.

(Twelfth night.)

IV.—TOUCHSTONE.

(As you like it.)

SECOND PERIOD.

The poet is now beginning to leave behind him the spirit of "clever youngmanishness," and to lay hold of the principles of life, to understand the purpose of the world, and of men; and he begins to deal with it in a very powerful way through his histories. "The compression of the age, and the rough matter of history into dramatic form, demanded the vigorous exercise of the plastic energy of the imagination; and the circumstance that he was dealing with reality and positive facts of the world, must have served to make clear to Shakspere that there was sterner stuff of poetry, material more precious—even for purposes of art—in active life, than could be found in the conceits, and prettinesses, and affections, which at times led him astray in his earlier writings." Still he did not start upon any profound enquiry concerning the deeper and more terrible problems of existence, so that this period of his clowns may be regarded as the freshest and most enjoyable. Their wit is genuine, and full of vivacity and truth, and it is striking that in almost all the plays of this period the musical element appears; Shakspere's laughter, therefore, could not be more clear and musical than it is now.

"ALL'S WELL THAT ENDS WELL."

Of this work little need be said; it is amongst our author's less genial plays, but it serves our purpose to mark the poet's transition from the florid and exaggerated style of wit to the more substantial English tone of the second period. Only the comic parts of the play—the characters of Parolles, Lafeu, the Clown, and the Countess—are the real property and invention of Shakspere. The Clown seems to think that his *forte* lies in the fit answering of every question put to him. He says of Parolles that "to say nothing, to know nothing, to have nothing, is to be a great part of your title, which is very little of nothing." The witticisms of this fool to Parolles, and such like cowards, are like "inopportune bullets," but to the generous and the guiltless who have a free conscience they are mere "bird-bolts"—the wit of the fool shoots vainly over their heads, whilst it discovers at once the folly of those who shrink at the whizzing of its arrows.

FESTE *(Twelfth Night)*.

The comic elements of *Twelfth Night* are again entirely Shakspere's own, and it has been called the purest and merriest comedy he has written. The play was intended for the night of the twelfth of December, the eve which ushers in the Carnival—the season in which at that day in England bean Kings were chosen by lot, merry court scenes were kept in family circles, and Masquerades for the purpose were performed in the theatres. For a mad season like this, mad jests are here represented as it were for choice *(what you will)*, and the play is full of sweetness, good-nature, and pleasantry. There is some satire but no spleen, it aims at the ludicrous rather than the ridiculous. Two strata of society are represented, characters of a more refined organization, and characters in which the vices of human nature grow luxuriantly as weeds. The poet hits out right and left at their follies, but he does not despise the characters nor bear them any ill-will, for "there is no slander in an allowed fool, though he do nothing but rail ; nor no railing in a known discreet man though he do nothing but reprove." *

We have to notice in Feste—for he deserves his name quite as much as Launcelot or Touchstone—one of the best creations of our poet : he dares for the first time to hold up before his hearers a fool of the first order, and of the most varied powers :—

> This fellow's wise enough to play the fool,
> And to do that well craves a kind of wit :
> He must observe their mood on whom he jests,
> The quality of persons, and the time,
> And, like the haggard, check at every feather
> That comes before his eye. This is a practice
> As full of labour as a wise man's art ;
> For folly, that he wisely shows, is fit,
> But wise men, folly laden, quite taint their wit.
> *Act III. Sc. iv. 64—72.*

He throws off the rudeness and vulgarity of Launcelot and Costard, and puts upon the stage a clown who dares to assert his powers and his superiority. Feste has a finger in everything throughout the piece : thinks himself at

---

* Act I. v. 90—92.

liberty to speak his mind upon every subject that comes
before his notice, and yet he is out of the reach of everybody, and through the sharpness of his wit he generally
gets the best of an argument. He is not only a humorist,
he is a singer, a witty entertainer, and a "corrupter of
words" as he calls himself. No other of Shakspere's Fools
has so shewn his superiority as this; in fact he says he is
no Fool at all, it is a great mistake to call him so, or to call
his foolish wisdom folly, for he avows that his brain is
nothing like so motley as his dress.

He is opposed in some way or other to every character in
the play, and the passage above quoted shows how well he
understood them all " to observe their mood on whom he
jests, the quality of persons, and the time." He studies all
his characters and his manner of speech to them—taking
care in the meantime always to ask for what he knows he
will get—knowing all their weaknesses, considering their
nature, adapting everything to the mood of the moment.
He searches to the depth of his mistress's sorrow, pene-
trates the destiny of Maria, and Sir Toby's weak *pia
mater*, "holds up the mirror to the opalescent humours
of the duke," and yet with all this he is a careless,
cheerful fellow, troubling himself about nothing,· placed
in the midst of this bustling company, " a wise fool
amongst the foolish wise." He thinks himself much
better off for his enemies than for his friends, for his
friends make an ass of him by praising him, but
his foes tell him plainly that he is an ass; so that
by his foes he profits in the knowledge of himself, and by
his friends he is abused. And he has a musical talent, which
is most diversified—" a most mellifluous voice, and a very

sweet and contagious breath." He appears as a singer by profession, and sings with equal skill love-songs of a merry or tragic nature to suit either the dreamy and poetical being of the duke, or the noisy company of Sir Toby, who shakes the house with his laughter, and calls up the straight-laced Malvolio at midnight. He says he takes pleasure in his singing, and refuses recompense : he deprecates expressly the idea of his begging being construed into covetousness.

He is most faithfully devoted to his mistress, and speaks with her as one belonging to her house ; he condemns the extravagance of her melancholy, and proves her foolish for mourning a brother, because he has gone to Heaven—a much better place. He promotes the connection between Viola and Sebastian, and is at once on a friendly footing with these naturally fresh and free natures. With Sir Andrew he talks glaring nonsense, because he knows it enchants him, and with Sir Toby he passes for no fox. They praise his personal appearance : " the fool has an excellent breast : I had rather than forty shillings I had such a leg and so sweet a breath to sing."* He watches the actions of Maria, and praises her as the most witty of her sex if she can win Sir Toby from drinking. But with Malvolio he cannot agree. Malvolio is an austere Puritan : his crossed garters distinguish him at once ; and he speaks with contempt of the fool and his profession. The fool's pride is at once wounded, and he joins readily enough in the trick to cure Malvolio of his self-conceit and, in the character of Sir Topas, plagues him till he is nigh mad indeed, and then leaves him in his misery.

* Act II., Sc. III., 9.

TOUCHSTONE *(As You Like It)*.

The two characters Jacques and Touchstone shew us a just view of the two kinds of life of which the play consists— that of the court, and that of the country. In the anecdotes, reflections, and declamations of these two, we have the corruptions of affected society brought into contact with woodland habits with remarkable force. Both are characters of the court, and of highly sophisticated society ; their actions and conversation partake largely of the court, and therefore few things under the greenwood tree are genial to them.

We have seen how, in the earlier comedies, the wit of the fools has been a mere play upon words, and given out almost unconsciously; but now the poet begins to invest his clowns with that prophetic vein they were said to possess, and to which the age gave credence. Touchstone is not quite so expert, nor so sensible of his wit as Feste, but he is of a more elevated nature : he stands on the doubtful limit of instinct and consciousness. Jacques says that he is a clown who has crammed the strange places of his dry brain with observation, " which he vents in mingled forms" ; he considers him one of those natural philosophers (natural fools) of whom Touchstone himself says they have learned no wit by nature nor art. He assumes the appearance of being wiser than he himself knew he was; he is " ne'er aware of his wit till he breaks his shins against it." Celia ascribes to him the dulness of the fool as the whetstone of his wit, while to the true fool the folly of others is the whetstone of wit. But he regards himself as far superior to the clown and the natural philosopher, which the duke readily perceives:

" he uses his folly like a stalking-horse, and under the presentation of that shoots his wit."

Touchstone recognises the analogies of court and country life, and makes fun of both. He comments with shrewd observation upon the coarseness and unhandsomeness of shepherd life, but he gives way soon enough to the influence of Audrey. He makes fun of the trivialities of court life in his stories of the courtier who swore on his honour when he had'nt any; he destroys at once all the courage and honour of the courtier in his famous account of the seven lies and his panegyric on the virtues of an *if :*—

> "The first, the retort courteous; the second, the quip modest; the third, the reply churlish; the fourth, the reproof valiant; the fifth, the countercheck quarrelsome; the sixth, the lie with circumstance; the seventh, the lie direct. All these you may avoid, but the lie direct; and you may avoid that, too, with an *if*. I knew when seven justices could not take up a quarrel; but when the parties were met themselves, one of them thought but of an *if*, as *if you said so, then I said so*; and they shook hands and swore brothers. Your *if* is the only peace-maker; much virtue in *if*."
>
> *Act V. iv. 90—103.*

And refined manners are also satirized in his conversation with Corin, who, he says, is cursed because he never was at court :

> "Why if thou never wast at court, thou never saw'st good manners; if thou never saw'st good manners, then thy manners must be wicked; and wickedness is sin, and sin is damnation. Thou art in a parlous state, Shepherd."
>
> *Act III. ii. 40—44.*

Touchstone takes things as he finds them, he criticizes them even more severely than Jacques, and he knows how to make the best of his opportunities. He is no longer a mere clown, he is one of Shakspere's faithful fellows; he follows his mistress into exile; he takes advantage of his court education to become a great figure amongst the rustics.

I

When he goes back to the court he will assume the airs of the forest in the servant's hall. Meanwhile he accepts either court or country, and acts in harmony with his surroundings, criticizing both without any spitefulness.

THIRD PERIOD.

Ab imo Pectore:
SOUL-STIRRING—CENSORIOUS—MAJESTIC.

I.—CHARACTERISTICS.
II.—THE GRAVE-DIGGERS.
(Hamlet.)
III.—KING LEAR'S FOOL.
(King Lear.)
IV.—THE WINTER'S TALE.

THIRD PERIOD.

This is the period of Shakspere's great tragedies. He had now ceased to care for tales of mirth and love, for the movement of history or the pomp of war; his son is now dead, and he has tasted of human sorrow; he is beginning to sound the depths of the human heart, to enquire into the darkest and saddest parts of human life, to study the great mysteries of evil. His humour is now more pathetic than it has ever been before, it is also tragic and terrible; we have no longer his pleasant unalloyed mirth, or bright and sparkling fancy; his whole thought seems to be concentrated upon the evil and folly in man's heart. Shakspere's art now attains its most intense, its deepest significance, the interpenetration of the humourous. the pathetic, and the tragic, is now complete.

The Fool in *King Lear* is the type of this period. Through him the poet seems to be looking down upon life from a point outside and above life "from which the whole appears as some monstrous farce-tragedy, in which all that is terrible is ludicrous, and all that is ludicrous terrible."*

THE GRAVE-DIGGERS (*Hamlet*).

The clowns in *Hamlet* are interesting to us because they perpetuate the memory of poor Yorick: "a fellow of infinite jest, of most excellent fancy." As Hamlet holds up his

---

* Dowden—"His mind and art."

skull, how many happy recollections of him are aroused—
"he hath borne me on his back a thousand times, and now
how abhorred by my imagination! my gorge rises at it.
Here hung these lips that I have kissed I know not how
oft. Where be your gibes now—your gambles—your songs
—your flashes of merriment that were wont to set the table
on a roar."* The Clowns, "these ancient gentlemen," as
they call themselves, have a very grim grotesqueness; they
meet like humourous jesters in the court of death,
connoisseurs in corpses, chroniclers of dead men's bones.
Their conversation is interesting and quaint, and has
perhaps something more than outward significance. There is
something particular in the sneer at "Crowner Quest's Law,"
it strikes at those stupid verdicts given in such cases which
had so many untender consequences centuries later. The
Clown attempts to draw a distinction, to discriminate
between voluntary and involuntary suicide :

"Here lies the water, good ; here stands the man, good ; if the man go to this
water and drown himself, it is, will he, nill he, he goes ; mark you that ; but if the
water come to him, and drown him, he drowns not himself ; argal, he that is not
guilty of his own death shortens not his own life."

Act V., Sc. i. 15—21.

They find fault with the fact that great folk should have
countenance in this world to hang or drown themselves
more than their even christians, and conclude with an
expression upon the high standing of their profession—there
are no ancient gentlemen but gardeners, ditchers, and
grave-diggers, they hold up Adam's profession, and he was
"the first man who bore arms."

* Act V., Sc. i. 191—200.

KING LEAR'S FOOL *(King Lear).*

This, the last Fool we shall notice, is the most important of our poet's creations. He is no buffoon "to make the groundlings laugh," and though he contributes much towards the relief of the heart-rending scenes, he is a most faithful fool, and is brought into living connection with the pathos of the play—a thing we have hitherto been unable to say. The first three acts of *King Lear* have been pronounced the great masterpieces of Shakspere in logic and passion. The heart of Lear is torn asunder by the "petrifying indifference, the cold calculating, obdurate selfishness of his daughters."* The sense of sympathy in the reader or listener to this uncontrollable anguish would be too painful to be borne but for the intervention of the fool, whose well-timed levity comes in to break the continuity of feeling when it can no longer be borne. Kent and the fool stick to Lear through all his misery, the one brings about his reunion with Cordelia, the other contrives by his jest to divert his ill-humour, and to keep him from madness. They both possess a mastery over nature and inclination: they put to shame the daughters of the old King by their faithful devotion to him. Kent suppresses his own indignation and sense of injury, and does all in his power to assist his master; the fool mockingly praises Kent for it, and offers him his cap and bells for such true service to the neglected man—"for taking one's part that's out of favour." The fool himself cleaves just as much to Lear, and carries on his jests with a heavy and care-worn heart, suppressing his own anguish with songs and jokes. He taunts Lear with

---

* Compare Shakspere's Hypocrites—Goneril and Regan.

having given away all that he has to his daughters: he is even worse off than a fool, who at the extremity can claim his coxcomb.   So he gives Lear a speech :—

> " Have more than thou showest,
> Speak less than thou knowest,
> Lend less than thou owest,
> Ride more than thou goest,
> Learn more than thou trowest,
> Set less than thou throwest."
>
> *Act I. v. 120—125.*

Lear had little wit in his crown when he gave his golden one away, and made his daughters his mothers :

> *Then they for sudden joy did weep,*
> *And I for sorrow sung,*
> *That such a king should play bo-peep,*
> *And go the fools among.*
>
> *Act I. v. 176—180.*

He is worse than a snail, which has a shell to put its head in—even this slow thing does not give his case away and leave his horns without a covering.   The King should not have grown old before he had grown wise, for by giving his fortune to his daughters, he had proved himself to have as little wit in his bald crown as there was in the empty crowns of two eggs.

After one of his daughters has turned him to the door Lear still takes heart, for he has yet another daughter who will treat him kindly; but the fool knows better than he— she is as like her sister as a crab is to an apple; and "winter's not gone yet if the wild geese fly that way :

> Fathers that wear rags
> Do make their children blind ;
> But fathers that bear bags,
> Shall see their children kind."
>
> *Act II. iv. 48—51.*

When Lear is finally turned out in the storm the fool is

still with him, his faithful follower, but continuing his taunts, trying to prevent Lear, as he thinks, from going mad.

It has been said that the fool by his wit does not alleviate the inward pangs, and outward woes of Lear, but that he rather augments them; from the first the fool's strokes at Lear's follies are beyond a joke: instead of distracting his thoughts, they drive him to dwell upon those which torture him; and however well his jests may serve the aesthetic end of not allowing the spectator to dwell too painfully and continually upon the violent outbursts of Lear's madness, they are on the other hand, psychologically considered, improper and injudicious as a remedy against this very malady.*   But considering the character as a work of art the fool is indispensable.   The storm scene would not be half so effective if his chatter and taunt were missing: we should fail to realize the physical strait to which Lear is reduced; "moral illustrations would equally be marred by his loss, for his mixture of affection, playfulness, wit, childishness, innocence, and triviality, corresponds with the chaotic disturbances of the King as he mingles raving with wisdom, and new discovered humanities, but with the difference of exemption from the stings of heartstruck anguish and self-reproach."   In another point also it is indispensable inasmuch as while it is a diversion to the too great intensity of our disgust, it carries the pathos to the highest possible pitch by showing the pitiable weakness of the old King's conduct, and its irretrievable consequences from the most familiar point of view.

* Gervinus—Shakspere Commentaries.

THE WINTER'S TALE.

At last, Shakspere passes out of this period of depression
and sorrow, and once again before his end attains the calm
serenity over the world; his mirth and humour is once more
bright and tender, and from this elevation he can pass again
into the simple merriment of rustic festivity; he can enjoy
the broad open-mouthed humour of the country clowns.

The impression left upon the reader by our poet's last
plays is, that whatever his trials and sorrows and errors may
have been, he comes forth from them wise, large-hearted,
calm-souled. He seems to have learned the secret of life,
and while taking his share in it, to be yet disengaged from
it; he looks down upon life, its joys, its griefs, its errors,
with a grave tenderness, which is almost pity. The spirit
of these last plays is that of serenity which results from
fortitude and the recognition of human frailty; all of them
express a deep sense of the need of repentance, and the duty
of forgiveness. And they all show a delight in youth and
the lovliness of youthful joy, such as one feels who looks on
these things without possessing them, or any longer desiring
to possess them. Shakspere in this period is most like his
own Prospero. In these "Romances," and in the "Frag-
ments," a supernatural element is present; man does not
strive with circumstances and with his passions in darkness; the gods preside over our human lives and fortunes,
they communicate with us by visions, by oracles, through
the elemental powers of nature. Shakspere's faith seems to
have been that there is something without and around our
human lives, of which we know little, yet which we know

to be beneficient and divine. He had ascended out of the turmoil and trouble of action, out of the darkness and tragic mystery, the places inhabited by terror and crime, and by love contending with these to a pure and serene elevation.*

University College of Wales,
    May, 1882.

---

* Dowden—Shakspere Primer p. 60.

STYLE AND THOUGHT.

"Style is the dress of thoughts; and let them be ever so just, if your style is homely, coarse, and vulgar, they will appear to as much disadvantage, and be as ill received, as your person, though ever so well proportioned, would, if dressed in rags, dirt, and tatters."—CHESTERFIELD.

STYLE AND THOUGHT.

"Le style est l'homme même—The style is the man."—BUFFON.

One of the finest, one of the most essential and important attainments to which we aspire is unquestionably that of being able to give expression to our thoughts in a suitable manner. We admire the orator who can entertain and instruct the crowd with his eloquence; we are inclined to envy the man who can enliven a social circle with his conversational powers; the painter and the musician are the objects, too, of our praise; but above all we honour the writer and the poet—he who can give to us his thoughts in a clear and intelligible manner; and we esteem him the more if he can combine with this all the beauty and elegance of his language. For we can read and meditate upon his sayings when those of the mere talker have long since been forgotten. Through him we hold converse with the great minds of the past, men continue to live after they are dead, and be felt as a power and presence in the earth; he unfolds to us the pages of history; he reveals to us the mysteries of science; and his work does not fade with the lapse of time, fine pictures drawn by the pen will

---

* For the full quotation from Buffon *vide* end of the Essay.

outlive the choicest specimens upon canvas. Choice sentences need no restoration ; they are safe from external influence, and even from the malicious pen of the critic. A gem of thought once set in words retains its lustre undiminished, and descends as a sacred heir-loom from generation to generation. Too much importance cannot be given to the habit of writing. It is a powerful means of expanding the mind, it braces the faculties, gives them strength and quickness, and is conducive to the systematic arrangement of our thoughts, views, and opinions. Original composi- has been aptly called "the enemy to self-deception," on account of the terrible disclosures it sometimes makes as to the crudeness of our conceptions, the treachery of our memory, the poverty of our knowledge, and our inability to express clearly even the little we know. Indeed we cannot hope to understand thoroughly the principles of any subject unless we habituate ourselves to expressing our thoughts upon that subject in writing.

This is an essay to prove the truth of Buffon's aphorism, "The style is the man."* Buffon here asserts that the style, the manner in which a writer's thoughts are presented, must essentially reveal the man : that when we become thoroughly acquainted with a writer's style, we get an insight into the man's nature—his truest self ; that we can form from this some estimate of the man's character, his attainments, his mode of thinking, his disposition, and perhaps his motives. The first question to consider, then, is what Buffon means here by style. He himself says, "Style supposes the union of all the intellectual

---

* Vide Forspeech.

faculties; to *write well* is at once to *think well*, to feel rightly, and to express properly; it is to have at the same time mind, soul, and taste." We assume, of course, that a man has something to say, for if he has nothing to say, certainly he had better hold his tongue. And even when he *has* something to say, it does not always follow that other men will give any attention unless there be something also in his mode of saying it. It is this which we have to consider—the manner, the style, in which a thought is expressed. And the style of an author depends upon many things; its laws are said by most Rhetoricans to be derived from custom—national, recent, and reputable. No doubt custom holds sway over the acceptance of new words, the rejection of obsolete forms, and other changes in language; and the most acceptable style is generally the one which reflects the sympathies of our own day; still it is not good style that makes reputable writers,—good writers make the style reputable. It follows then that the real regulation of style is the genius of the language, and a man can only form a good style by earnest attention to this one thing alone. After the imperative laws of accuracy and purity in the selection of words has been complied with, the rest—perspicuity, strength, grace, and all the excellencies of a good author, must necessarily depend upon the man, and the attention he has given to it. For it has been wisely asserted that whatever be the characteristic of a good style, it must have been attained at some time or other by earnest labour and perseverance. An author must make style an object; it must be his own, and it must be natural and simple; but, to be his own, it must be formed by the study of other men's; and to be natural and simple, it must be

K

gradually acquired by long devotion to composition as an
art. For one has little faith in inspirations and impulses,
that is, as the means of bringing a man's style to perfection,
though we know well their use in starting what labour
must elaborate.

In this way a man's style becomes himself—by the degree
of labour he has bestowed upon it. By this long and
patient service he comes to send out his compositions
marked and modified by whatever is his; it cannot but be
marked by whatever belongs to him; it will betray his
weakness, it will indicate his strength; it flows from his
temperament if it be peculiar; it is coloured by his genius,
if he has any. Passion and earnestness, vigour or timidity,
anything powerful or predominant in the man will make
themselves felt in his style. It is like his walk, his step,
his tone of voice, his manners, his dress, or anything else
which, as an outward, visible sign, embodies and reveals the
inward life.*

We can, therefore, say that an author's style is one of
the best criterions of his mind and his temperament—we
can judge of the quality of a thought by the manner in
which it is given. One critic might say, "it was a good
idea;" another might say, "it was well put;" but where is
the difference between the two? Is there any? Are not
the expressions simply two ways of saying the same thing?
Is not the effect of the idea owing to the manner in which
it is put? The thought and the style are, therefore, so
closely allied as to be inseparable: the style being the
representation, the sign of the thought, it must reveal the

---

* *Vide* Binney's lecture on "Authorship" (Exeter Hall series).

degree in which a writer has comprehended his subject. If he expresses himself in a vague and general manner, he has but a vague and general idea of his subject. If on the other hand he is clear and exact, he has in a corresponding degree clearly and exactly realized his thought. These, then, are the grounds upon which it is maintained that Buffon was correct in saying, " The style is the man."

The principal objection to this contention is that it is not the style which reveals the man, but the *thought* which the style represents ; that the style is simply the outward mark of the inward feeling. At first sight there appears to be much reason in this theory, but after consideration it must give way, for how are we to know what a man's thoughts are apart from his style ? A writer always strives to express himself as well as he can,—if he does not, we are not bound to give him credit for knowing something he does not express,—therefore, if the style be a true representation of the thought, the style is the thought, and the thought is the style : they cannot be separated. If a thought has not been sufficiently understood, then the style must be obscure, if on the other hand the thought has been perfectly conceived; the style is clear and intelligible. What is the distinguishing feature of our great writers—in what does their excellence consist ? Is it not in their manner of putting things quite as much as the things themselves ? The same ideas have been expressed by different writers in as many different ways, but why is it that one is read with so much more pleasure and interest than another ? Simply because the idea, or the sentiment, has been felt, thought out, and understood by the one in a much greater degree than the other. Here is one writer who is content with presenting his thoughts in the barest possible form : his style is dry and unattractive, and we have no pleasure in reading it. Another expresses himself in a very general manner; his words are uncertain ; his ideas seem loose and undecided, so that we can scarcely conceive his meaning. A third surrounds his thought with such a mass of verbiage that we have great difficulty in finding the meaning at all. But a really good writer presents his ideas in so clear a manner that we can follow him with ease, and consequently with pleasure. He is careful to use no term which will not be understood, while at the same time he combines all the virtues of orna ment without any of its excesses. Such care has been dis played in the selection of words that they are alike pleasing to the eye, and harmonious to the ear. The differences of style simply reveal the degree in which the thought has been realized ; in every case " the style is the man."

Another objection urged is that an author often borrows his style from another, writes exactly in the same strain, and imitates his master in every particular. Surely, it is said, this writer cannot reveal his character in his style ? But if one writer adopts the style of another it shews that the style of the one attracts the other ; that the thoughts of both run in the same groove. If therefore we know the style of the one imitated, we can judge of the character of the imitator. We shall thus not only get at the clue to his nature, we shall also prove him to be devoid of originality.

A further remark we often hear when an opinion is being given upon the style of a writer is that " the thought is good, but the style is bad." From what has already been said, it is evident that this is a mistake : if the thought had been good, the style would have been good. In such cases the one who criticizes perhaps comprehends the thought more clearly than the writer himself. Then there is the case of obscure style. This may result from over-condensation; a writer may have become so familiar with his own thoughts that he is not considerate enough in expressing them, consequently they are obscure to the reader. Obscurity in style, however, is oftener the result of obscurity in thought, and a man can scarcely claim to have thought more clearly than he speaks.

In order to illustrate the correctness of Buffon's assertion, let us endeavour to show the main characteristics of some of our great writers as revealed in their style. To commence with Shakespeare, the greatest of all poets. He has been justly called " the poet of nature." In his writings we have a faithful mirror of manners and of life. He gives us pictures of characters of almost every type, from the purest virtue to the deepest villany. All this shews us that he had a most intimate acquaintance with human nature, that he was a keen observer of man and his surroundings, that he understood the human character in all its phases, and in such a manner as to have few equals, if any. Chaucer, too, shews us that he had a wide acquaintance with every phase of the society of his day, that he was highly humorous, and so vigorous in his description as to have few rivals. Milton reveals to us in his poetical productions the calm tranquility of his character, and the purity of his life; they shew us that his mind was lofty and vigorous, though he was almost devoid of passion and sympathy; that his imagination was rich and fertile, while his sentiments were of the sublimest character. Spenser discloses in his " Fairy Queen " an imagination of the widest dimensions; while Burns shews us that he delighted in giving expression to feelings which everyone has experienced, and in language which everyone can understand. Style tells us that Cowper was amiable and pious, though rendered wretched by mental disease; that Byron was given to habits of indulgence, but at the same time he possessed a kind and generous heart. The style of Addison indicates an elegant and an accomplished mind; that he was dignified and polished, and that he was gifted with a delicate and lively fancy. The purity of the pages of Sir Walter Scott is ample evidence of his good manners, and religious principles, and shews his great regard for the feelings of others.

If then, style and thought are inseparable, to study style is to stimulate thought; and perhaps we are apt to forget the latter fact. We may think that simply the reading and copying of the "masters of style" are sufficient, for we know that it is much easier to imitate than to be original—it saves the trouble of thinking out a subject. If we thought and wrote more, we should have less to fear about the style. Southey contends that a man with "a clear head, a good heart, and an honest understanding, will always write well. It is owing either to a muddled head, an evil heart, or a sophisticated intellect, that men write badly, and sin against their reason, or goodness, or sincerity." A good thought, then, will find good expression, the mind will be satisfied with nothing less; a clear idea will find utterance in clear words. If words fail to present themselves to the mind, the idea has not been fully realized, and proper words must be sought for. We have been told that whatever we do in attempts at writing, to always do our best, because the results depend upon this—results both

as to solid advantage and to safe and allowable delight.
We must work on the substance of our thoughts—their
order and cohesion; we must see that they are just, true,
full, select—accurately arranged, artistically so, to awaken
interest or secure impression. We must labour also at
something more than merely expressing them—expressing
them so as to make them intelligible. We are assured that
severe, painstaking, prolonged effort, thus directed, will
have its reward—a manifold reward. Time spent in testing
terms, in moulding sentences, in observing the shades and
colours of words, in finding out synonymous or parallel
expressions, in forming the ear to harmony and rhythm, in
compelling it to listen for the march and cadence, and to
become sensible to the niceties of measure and modulation;
time thus spent will not only not be lost, but will be rich
in enjoyments of no common order. Then, always doing
our best, we shall soon learn to do things well; our power
over words will increase; habit will give facility and
command; the style will be formed; when we sit down to
write we shall easily find fitting phraseology: words will
obey the first call, and take their places without effort.
We must remember "that no man who writes for posterity
can afford to neglect the art of composition. The trimmer
bark, though less richly laden, will float farther down the
stream of time; and when so many authors of real ability
and learning are competing for every niche in the temple of
fame, *the coveted place will assuredly be won by style.** "
We take these latter remarks most earnestly to heart, and
trust every reader will similarly apply them.

University College of Wales, November, 1879.

* *Vide* Essays from the *Times.*

This article appeared in *The Journalist** of February, 1880, and the following month "A Rejoinder" appeared from the pen of a writer to that magazine, who says that the remarks upon "Style and Thought" had come into violent collision with his pre-conceived notions with regard to the means for acquiring a good style. He maintains that the aphorism, "The style is the man," can be only partially true; and the statement that "when we become thoroughly acquainted with a man's style we are introduced to his truest self," is open to serious question. A man might give accurate and elegant expression to noble and pure thoughts, whilst in heart and life he was the veriest scoundrel. He thinks that the drift of the whole article is that "if you wish to write English well, all you had to do is to make yourself a great thinker, as great thoughts and noble ideas cannot possibly be expressed in incorrect or weak language." He says the best answer to this is the following extract † :—

"Consider," says our Lord, "the lilies, how they grow : they toil not, they spin not; and yet I say unto you that Solomon, in all his glory, was not arrayed like one of these. If, then, God so clothe the grass, which is to-day in the field, and to-morrow is cast into the oven, how much more will he clothe you."

He then quotes one of the tasteless modern paraphrases—

"Consider the flowers, how they gradually increase in size : they do no manner of work, and yet I declare unto you, that nothing whatever, in his most splendid habit, is dressed like them. If, then, God in his providence so adorn the vegetable productions, which continue but for a little on the land, and are afterwards put into the fire, how much more will he provide clothes for you?"

Here, he says, are the same sentiments expressed in different language, and the obvious deduction from them would be,

---

* *The Journalist*—a London shorthand magazine, published monthly.
† From Cambell's "Philosophy of Rhetoric," Vol. ii., pp. 137.

not that the one was a good thinker, and the other a poor
one, but that the one had a thorough command of terse,
epigrammatic English, whilst the other was encumbered with
a round-aboutness of expression and a diffuseness and infla-
tion which could only be remedied by an earnest, incessant
study of good authors, and a constant endeavour to find the
most appropriate words for not only the noblest but the most
trivial thoughts. He further maintains that there is no force
at all in the statement that the man who imitates another's
style would necessarily be devoid of originality. It was well
known that Junius formed his style largely on that of Johnson; that Franklin acquired his singularly clear and simple
style by reading the *Spectator*, and writing and re-writing some
of its best papers; that when Clarendon was writing his history he was constantly studying Livy and Tacitus, to acquire
the full, flowing style of the one, and the portraiture of the
other; that Demosthenes copied Thucydides' History eight
times;—and who would say that these had no originality?
In the writer's opinion, "the best way to acquire a good
style is to make yourself thoroughly acquainted with the
grammatical forms of your language, and then, dictionary
in hand, give your days and nights to the study of the
language of the best authors."

The following is a summary of the reply which was
made to the foregoing remarks. The writer of the rejoinder
had drawn an absolute distinction between Thought and
Style, and contended that we could consider the one apart
from the other. But no such distinction could be drawn—
they were inseparable—inasmuch as the style was only the
representation of the thought, the style revealed exactly
the degree in which the writer had understood his subject.
Certainly a writer *might* give elegant expression to noble
thoughts, and be at the same time a scoundrel; but such
characters could only form very miserable exceptions to the
general rule. Standard writers followed their best
impulses in all they wrote : their work was the outcome of
their inward, their truest nature—the vibrations of their
very souls. The quotations from "Campbell's Rhetoric"
were rather arguments in support of the aphorism ; but the
two passages were not "two ways of expressing the same
idea." "Consider the lilies of the field how they grow,"

was not the *same* thing as "Consider the flowers how they gradually increase in size." They approached each other in meaning, but the author of the one had fully realized his thought, the other only partially so; the one expressed precisely what he meant, the other something like it. Then, to have "a thorough command of terse and epigrammatic language," a man must be possessed with a mind capable of grasping and appreciating terse and figurative ideas, whilst "to be encumbered with a round-aboutness of expression" was to be burdened with a slow roundabout method of thought. The passages quoted were ample proof that the "author of one was a good thinker, and the other a bad one." To illustrate this the following statement was made :—it would be admitted that language was only the sign for ideas, or as Emerson put it, "all language is fossil language." Language had developed with man's intellect; as man noticed things around him he named them according to their most striking attributes. But in time the attributes of one class of things became applied to another class, and by this association of terms, words had come to have a different meaning to that originally intended. Thus, great confusion and ambiguity had arisen, and many words usually called synonymes were not really so: a close examination would shew that in the majority of cases there was a shade of difference in their meaning. Now, the great difficulty, in English composition, was to find out the word which expressed exactly—nothing more and nothing less—what we meant. With most unpracticed writers the word which presented itself most readily was not the one we wanted, hence we had to find another. Therefore, the contention was that the words by which we expressed ourselves, revealed exactly the degree of excellence we had attained in the thought. The writer of the rejoinder must have misunderstood the statement that the author who imitated another must be devoid of originality, though he did not prove the statement to be false by the examples he quoted. The eminent writers mentioned did not imitate in the sense of the word intended, they rather sought to make themselves thoroughly acquainted with their favourite author's mode of thinking, or with his style, which was the same thing. The meaning of the original assertion was, that lavish and minute imitation practiced by some which left no margin for the exercise of their own thoughts. The distinction between the two kinds of imitation was exactly the same as that between two painters visiting a gallery of the great masters—one with canvass under his arm, brush in hand, and a determination to *make a copy;* the other taking nothing but himself, to study the *manner* in which the great artists represented nature in all her varied beauty by means of her colours. There was certainly no other way to acquire a good style than by the "earnest and incessant study of good authors, and this would surely make us good thinkers too. We should strive to get at the meaning of the words conveyed, and then noble thoughts would not be "expressed in weak and ineffective language." There was often the danger to dress up common place ideas in pompous terms, but it was generally the least effective, besides being extremely silly, and only exposing the writer to ridicule. If we carefully thought out what we really wanted to say, and then said it in plain language, we should do something far worthier—for without simplicity, clearness, and precision, all ornaments, however elegant, would only glimmer through the darkness.

University College of Wales,
April, 1880.

The following is a translation from Buffon, on the subject of style in the *Encyclopédie ;* *vide* Dr. Ethé's article in *The University College of Wales Magazine,* May, 1882:—

"Style is nothing else but the order and movement which we bring into our thoughts ; if we put them into narrow fetters, if we condense them, the style becomes firm, vigorous, and concise ; if we let them loose, if we allow them to follow one another slowly, and to join only at the favour and liberty of the words, however elegant these may be, the style will turn out a diffuse, lax and languid one. But before we seek the order in which we will present our thoughts, we must have formed another more general and more regular order, into which we admit only the first genuine views and the principal ideas ; only by marking out their place on the basis of this preliminary plan a subject can become circumscribed, and we can learn its real extent. This preliminary plan is not yet the style, but it is the foundation of the style ; it supports it, directs it, regulates its movements, submits it to fixed laws. Without that the best writer loses his way, his pen moves along without a guide, and puts down at random irregular strokes and discordant figures. However brilliant the colours may be he uses, however numerous the beauties he scatters throughout the details, the whole building will be badly constructed, will be either too impressive, offensive to sight, or not impressive enough, and in admiring the spirit of the author we will easily suspect that he lacks genius! It is the want of a plan, it is the fault of not having reflected enough on his subject, that a highly gifted man feels embarrassed and does not know where to commence to write. He perceives a vast number of ideas at once, and as he has neither compared nor subordinated them beforehand, nothing determines him to give one the preference over the other; he remains, therefore, perplexed. But when, on the other hand, he has made a plan, when he has once gathered and arranged all those thoughts which are essential to his subject, he will easily become aware of the proper moment and the right place, when and where to begin; he will have a presentiment of the point of maturity in the productions of genius, he will be forced fairly and fully to develope it, and he will write with pleasure—ideas will follow without difficulty one after the other, and his style will become natural and easy. An ardent fire will grow out of this feeling of pleasure, it will spread everywhere, and imbue with life every expression; all will become more and more animated, all objects will assume colour, and sentiment joined to knowledge will increase it, will carry it further and further, will lead over from what has just been said to what the author is about to say, and the style will be at once interesting and luminous. To write well means indeed to think well, to feel well, and to represent well; it means to have at the same time spirit, soul, and good taste. The style, in short, implies both the combination and the practice of all intellectual faculties."

THE DECLINE OF THE DRAMA.

"*Action* is eloquence; and the *eyes* of the ignorant more learned than their *ears*."

SHAKSPERE.

THE DRAMA: ITS DECLINE AND REFORMATION.

We strive to give expression to our thoughts in different ways. Unfettered by formality, and prompted by impulse, we reveal our sympathies through different channels. By no means the least important of these is that of *Action*, for we may think, and speak, and write, but, after all, our actions reveal us most faithfully. Action is the highest perfection of our nature, it is the noblest pursuit of living. We influence those around us far more by our conduct than by our words,—though our speech betokens the kind of conduct to be expected of us. We also strive to imitate the good actions of others, to shape our lives after the lives from which those actions emanate. This desire is inherent in our nature ; our whole life is occupied with it.: it is the sport of infancy, the attraction of youth, and the aspiration of manhood. It was this desire which gave rise to the drama, that kind of poetry which seeks to imitate human nature : to tell a story of it by means of action.* The

* "Watch your children play, and you will see that almost their first conscious effort is to act and to imitate. It is an instinct, and you can no more repress it than you can extinguish thought. When this instinct of all is developed by cultivation in the few it becomes a wonderful art, priceless to civilisation in the solace it yields, the thought it generates, the refinement it inspires. Some of its latest achievements are not unworthy of their grandest predecessors. Some of its youngest devotees are at least as proud of its glories and as anxious to preserve them as any who have gone before. Theirs is a

promoters of the earlier, and the ruder kind of drama were
sensible of the fact that what is seen with the eyes makes a
deeper impression than what is heard with the ears. Action
is, therefore, the most important of the three dramatic
unities; the term drama signifies this,—and however much
it may differ in variety, and whatever dispute there may be
with regard to the unities of time and place, all are agreed
as to the unity of *action*.

The Drama occupies a singular position amongst the arts.
On the one hand it is by far the most natural, while on the
other it is the most artificial. Music imitates nature in
sound; painting seeks to picture her varied beauty by
means of her colours; language represents her in words;
while sculpture shews us her nobleness in form; but in the
drama all these characteristics are united. All the appar-
atus of stage machinery, the employment of actors, and the
like, bring it more into contact with external life than any
other form of imitation. On the other hand, the drama is
more idealistic, and much more complicated than any other
art. Its business is to portray the human character, it has
to do with man's nature, with his sympathies and passions,
and it treats of them with much more vigour than any
other kind of poetry, its characters speaking in blank verse.
The great difficulty, however, has always been to preserve
the balance between these two great principles. This was
most successfully accomplished in the Elizabethan age, when
a series of great ideas filled the minds of the whole people,

glorious heritage ! You honour it. They have a noble, but difficult
and sometimes a disheartening task. You encourage it. And no
word of kindly interest or criticism dropped in the public ear from
friendly lips goes unregarded or is unfertile of good ; and all criticism
is welcome."—HENRY IRVING.

when a true national feeling existed amongst them. At the end of this period, however, a disruption between the two sides commenced, and it became gradually divorced from the most earnest feeling of the country, and since then it has not been able to succeed. But before speaking of the causes which have led to this gradual decline in the Drama, it will be necessary to trace briefly its progress to the height of its power in the Elizabethan age.

The ruder kind of drama was introduced into our country mainly through the efforts of the clergy. Their representations consisted chiefly of events taken from the New Testament, and in the history of the Church. They were called "Miracle plays," and the clergy preferred this more effective method of imparting scriptural lessons to preaching sermons. But, with the philosophy of the mediæval ages, a change was brought about. This philosophy "dealt much in abstract terms, and delighted in definitions and logical distinctions." It was reflected in the "Moral plays" now introduced in which personages representing abstract ideas, such as Mercy, Truth, and Justice, were portrayed. In one sense they were a great advance upon the "Miracles," as they sought to convey sound moral lessons; and also gave occasion to some poetical and dramatic ingenuity in delineating such qualities, and assigning proper speeches to each. On the other hand, the scriptural personages being "refined away into mere moral abstractions," we lost altogether the portrayal of *real* character. The dulness of these plays, however, was not long tolerated, the miscellaneous audiences which attended them soon became tired of the serious subjects of the plays, and demanded that some pleasant mirth should be intermingled. The introduction of comic characters was the

L

result, and in many of the plays of this period they are thrust in at the most inopportune times. They appeared to think that no piece was complete unless the clown took a prominent part. About the same time historical personages were introduced, and frequently satire was employed. It had now been found that a human being, with a human name, was much better calculated to awaken the sympathies of an audience, to keep alive their attention, and to enforce moral truths, than a mere impersonation of an idea of the mind.

From this the genuine drama took its rise, and the progress it made, together with the large ideas which it originated, called forth many writers,—it attracted the very best men of the age. Hence it is that the Elizabethan period is by far the mightiest in the history of English Literature. Amongst the earlier writers of this age were the dramatists, Greene, Peele, and Marlowe; and they prepared, in some measure, the way for one who was to give to the drama its highest character. It became more classical in form, and took a prominent place in our national literature. The stage was adorned with more variety of character and action, and truer poetry. Above all the public ear became familiarised with blank verse, and this was, perhaps, the greatest improvement, for even "the genius of Shakspere would have been cramped and confined, had it been condemned to move in fetters of rhyme." But to Shakspere belongs the glory of having given the drama its model, its most natural form. In him the people were introduced to such real excellence that they were more disposed to wonder than to admire, to adore than to criticise. His remarkable power of imitating nature, his wonderful skill in portraying the human character, distinguishes him from the dramatists of his own age, or, indeed of any age. His characters range through almost every type of humanity, and furnish admirable subjects for the highest forms of the dramatic art. Along this path he pointed the future of the English Drama, and it could not henceforth depart from that path without being untrue to itself, and to its principles. He extended its empire to limits as yet unrecognised, and invested it with a splendour hitherto unknown. With a subservient pulpit and no press, it became the chief censor, the great critic, and satirist of the realm. The people were united by a great national feeling over the large ideas of the Renaissance; everyone who went to the theatre was a participator in the movement; their curiosity was awakened, their ideas of life were elevated, and altogether the drama exercised an influence upon the English nation not often recognised.

Unfortunately, however, the drama did not go further upon the path of progress. With the Reformation the people cooled down over the great ideas we have mentioned, and the bond of union in the nation passed away with them. Rivals to the drama sprung up in the shape of "Court masks," and the theatrical public were tempted aside. Writers for the stage began to shrink from the path laid down by their champion; they ceased to let their inward impulse guide them, and began pandering to the tastes of the people. The most vulgar jokes, and over-strained fantasies, were thrust upon the stage where Shakspere had placed characters with real life and passions. The tone of the drama became so low that the Puritans had no option in opposing it. They were instrumental in having the representation of stage plays prohibited on Sundays. The theatres were closed altogether during the plague of 1637, and the Puritans would have kept them so had that been possible; in fact they would have denied the people all amusements. These proceedings provoked a counter action in the minds of the public, and led to a more shameful degeneracy in the plays written for the stage. If the Puritans had sought to purify the stage performances, they would have conferred a lasting benefit on the nation, but their narrow views of life gave rise to a spirit which has occupied the mind of the middle classes of England from that day to the present.

The drama of the Restoration was still more immoral in its character than the Elizabethan in its final stage. Charles II. introduced the " Heroic plays," which were mostly founded on French and Spanish Romances. The themes were chiefly Love and Honour; they abounded in fine language, and were placed upon the stage in the most brilliant style; they were, however, altogether devoid of natural passion, and propriety of character. The nation had become still more divided in its opinion, and the drama was made to reflect the sympathies of its patrons, the court, and those inhabitants of the town who had court sympathies. These opinions were very narrow, and the class of people who held them were not distinguished by any earnestness of thought, or purpose in life. Hence the drama became of this character, all its power and wit were employed in the interest of vice, and it is much to be deplored that the great talents of Dryden were the most instrumental in extending this depraved national taste. But in time the models of the Heroic plays were worn out, and the French comedy took their place. The genius of Garrick also added fresh attractions to the stage in the earlier part of the eighteenth century. The introduction of the Italian opera, however, at the close of that century, almost absorbed what vitality remained in the drama. Its tone and manners were still further lowered by the religious re-action against it. It did not represent the more earnest feeling in the country, and on that ground it could not succeed.

The history of the drama in the present century has been one of gradual decline. In the earlier part, the prose writings of Scott, and the poetry of Byron satisfied, to a great extent, the imaginative demands of the public, and the attention of the cultivated classes was diverted from the drama. The spread of cheap literature also furnished intellectual entertainment for the people at home, and at a much cheaper rate than by attendance at the theatre. Dramatic compositions no longer occupy the prominent place they held in the literature of former periods of our history ; in fact it has been said that we have no modern drama at all. The love of spectacle and scenic display has gradually usurped its place, and the growth of this kind of entertainment has been the result. The theatrical performances of to-day are a mixture of almost every species of entertainment : a huddling together of tragedy, comedy, farce, melodrama, and spectacle. Consequently the performances are bad, and people are not unreasonably dissatisfied with them. Occasionally an attempt is made at Shakspere's plays, but, with the exception of the first-class performances in London, he is often utterly misrepresented. " What havoc they make of him, to be sure !" as Cibber puts it, "he is defaced and tortured in every single character ; Hamlet and Othello in one single hour loose all their goodness, and their sincerity; Brutus and Cassius become noisy blunderers, with bold, unmeaning eyes, mistaken sentiments, and turgid elocution."

It is noticeable that few dramas of our own day have met with much success when placed upon the stage, notwithstanding that we have some superior intellects engaged in them. The reason, however, is not an accidental one. Successful writing for the stage requires a close connection with the theatre itself, in order that the author may be able to adapt the language, the characters, the scenery, and the general structure of the piece, to the circumstances. The dramatists of the Elizabethan age, including their leader, were either themselves players, or maintained a close connection with the stage; hence their dramas are thoroughly *acting* dramas, and much more real than those of the modern school. At the present day, the two fundamental principles—the natural and the artificial— of the drama are too widely separated. Great writers will not subject themselves to a schooling from the actors, nor bend to a consideration of theatrical convenience. The consequence is, that they have either abstained altogether from dramatic composition, or written only what are termed "Dramatic Poems," the effect of which, being removed altogether from external circumstances, is quite incomparable with that produced by the true acting drama. We have had of late many adaptations from the French, which are, no doubt, masterpieces, so far as they portray *French* life and manners, but they are ridiculous when placed on an English stage; the sentiments expressed in them are too fantastical to appeal with any force to an English audience. Nevertheless, the visit of the French company to London, a short time ago, taught us a lesson in fine acting, and shewed us what could be done with a properly organised, and a national drama.

The growth of the critical spirit in the country has also materially lessened the interest which was once taken in the drama. Men prefer writing novels, in which they can stand aloof and talk about their characters—describe their actions and criticize them, while the Dramatist must make his characters speak and act for themselves.

The success of the drama has been further prevented by the action of the middle class of our nation towards it. From the days of Puritanism to the present, they have kept aloof from it, and that solely on the plea of its evil associations ; to give it their patronage would be inconsistent with their moral principles, and antagonistic to proper conduct in life. But, while it is admitted that the theatre has its immoral tendencies, our middle classes are by no means exonerated from blame in the matter. It is to a great extent owing to their narrow-mindedness that the drama has been allowed to degenerate so shamefully. If, instead of forsaking the theatre altogether, they had insisted upon having its purity maintained, the stage performances of to-day would have been something different. But they chose to enter "the prison of Puritanism, and had the key turned upon the spirit of the Drama for two hundred years." Happily, a change is now coming over them. They are beginning to see that all things in this life cannot be looked upon from one standpoint ; they must be viewed from several at the same time. They are beginning to feel that many things which go to ennoble the human character have been sacrificed to their narrow-mindedness, and amongst these they see the drama. A cry for its re-organisation is the result, and of late much progress has been made in this direction.

But there is a great barrier in the way of this re-establishment of a national drama, for such it must become if it is to succeed. We have no real national unity with regard to manners and life, as in the Elizabethan age. There is no real bond of thought, nor unity of feeling in the nation; party is divided against party, so that the drama at present can only appeal to a fragment of the whole people; it can only reflect the sympathies of a few. If we can revive this national unity, we can have a great national drama; and we have everything in England to bring about this result; all the elements are within our reach if we can only use them. We have the splendid national drama of the Elizabethan age, and a later drama which has no lack of pieces, "conspicuous for their stage qualities, their vivacity and talent, and interesting by their pictures of manners." We have also not a few good actors, led by one who is, in every sense of the word, worthy of that position—Mr. Henry Irving.* He is imbued with a sense of the import-

---

* "The universal study of Shakspere in our public schools is a splendid sign of the departure of prejudice; but it is acting chiefly that can open to others, with any spark of Shakspere's mind, the means of illuminating the world. Only the theatre can realise to us in a life-like way what Shakspere was to his own time. And it is, indeed, a noble destiny for the theatre to vindicate in these later days the greatness which sometimes it has seemed to vulgarise. It has been too much the custom to talk of Shakspere as nature's child—as the lad who held horses for people who came to the play— as a sort of chance phenomenon who wrote these plays by accident and unrecognised. How supremely ridiculous! How utterly irreconcilable with the grand dimensions of the man! Imagine him rather, as he must have been, the most notable courtier of the Court—the most perfect gentleman who stood in the Elizabethan throng—the man in whose presence divines would falter and hesitate lest their knowledge of the Book should seem poor by the side of

ance of the drama to national life and and manners, and he has done much towards awakening the interest which is now being taken in it. But in the work of re-organization, the theatre must be entirely separated from the great number of amusements which have for a long time accompanied it ; it must be cultivated alone as an art. It must return to the path laid down for it by its champion. and become a true representation of the life and manners of the time. It is a matter of great importance, as the progress of a nation depends as much upon its recreations as upon its labours. The re-organisation of the drama is, therefore, a work which ought to have the attention of every thoughtful Englishman.

University College of Wales,
March, 1880.

his, and at whom even queenly royalty would look askance, with an oppressive sense that here was one to whose omnipotent and true imagination the hearts of kings and queens and peoples had always been an open page. The thought of such a man is an incomparable inheritance for any nation, and such a man was the actor—Shakspere. Such is our birthright and yours. Such the succession in which it is ours to labour and yours to enjoy. For Shakspere belongs to the stage for ever, and his glories must always inalienably belong to it. If you uphold the theatre honestly, liberally, frankly, and with wise discrimination, the stage will uphold in future, as it has in the past, the literature, the manners, the morals, the fame, and the genius of our country. There must have been something wrong, as there was something poignant and lacerating, in prejudices which so long partly divorced the conscience of Britain from its noblest pride, and stamped with reproach, or at least depreciation, some of the brightest and world-famous incidents of her history." — HENRY IRVING, *before the Edinburgh Philosophical Institution, November, 1881.*

J. GIBSON, "CAMBRIAN NEWS" PRINTING WORKS, ABERYSTWYTH.